VÄNDRA

a novel

Enn Raudsepp

This is a work of fiction. Names, characters, places, and incidents are either the product of the author's imagination or are used fictitiously. Any resemblance to actual persons, living or dead, is entirely coincidental.

LAKESHORE PRESS

Printed in the United States of America

For K.R., E.M. and M.F., who lived through it all.

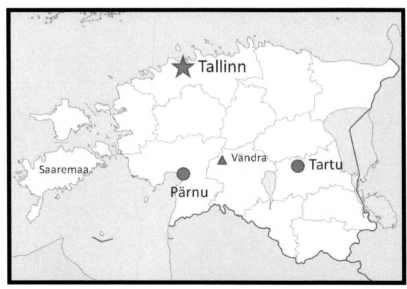

Prologue

In the geographical heart of the small Baltic country of Estonia lies a vast forest of oak, birch and pine surrounded by extensive boglands and traversed by the many tributaries of the Pärnu River, the country's longest. From the onset of the 13th Century, its dense groves have been a refuge for disaffected Estonians, the first of whom were uprooted by the Northern Crusade called by Pope Celestine III to Christianize the last outposts of paganism in northern Europe.

Latvia fell first and the soldier-monks under Bishop Albert of the Livonian order of Brothers of the Sword moved northwards to Estonia, where Lembit led the resistance for nine years before being killed in battle in 1217. Lembit, the first Estonian to have his name recorded by history, was secretly buried near his hill fort south of Vändra by priests of the Druidic MaaUsk, the pantheistic religion of the early Estonians.

In 1290, after years of fighting, King Valdemar II of Denmark annexed the northern coastal areas of Estonia and conceded the lands south of Vändra to the Livonian Brothers of the Sword.

The occupiers built stone castles and fortified manor houses, and prospered by imposing heavy taxes and work duties on the local population, who also suffered from forced conversions and tithing by the church.

The Estonians made a last desperate attempt to regain their freedom on St. George's night in 1343. Thousands were slaughtered in the bloody uprising, which lasted for two years before the Teutonic knights prevailed. The decimation of Estonia's traditional leaders, both secular and religious, left the country at the mercy of foreign invaders for nearly six centuries.

The rebels, resisters and runaway serfs who survived fled to the almost impenetrable forests of Vändra, the no-man's land separating the Danish and German fiefdoms, to live as outlaws. Not until the aftermath of World War One were the Estonians able to throw off the yoke of foreign domination, but only briefly, before falling once again to Soviet invaders.

VÄNDRA

a novel

Chapter One

The Reverend Karl Kingsepp sighed as he looked out the window before sinking back into his armchair in the book-lined rectory office. He hadn't had many good days lately, and had looked forward to spending two or three quiet hours with *The Brothers Karamazov*. He had thrown the windows wide open, and moved his armchair so that he could read in the warm afternoon sunshine. But he had barely picked up the book when Hilda Soosaar, his part-time secretary, stepped in with a disturbing message. The local commissar, Major Yüri Zhukov, would be dropping by in half-an-hour. No, he had not given a reason for his visit, Miss Soosaar said, causing the pastor no small degree of trepidation, though he tried to hide his unease. She would be going now, she told him, unless of course, he needed her to stay. "Ah no," he told her, forcing a slight smile. "I'm sure it's just some routine matter."

But after she left, he put the book aside, having lost all interest in reading. He felt his mouth going dry and his heartbeat quickening. Was this going to be it? He cast his eyes around the tidy office, remembering how happy he had been five years ago when he had sat down for the first time at the old pastor's desk. The office had looked very different then, all dark wood, very plain, verging on the shabby, but it was his! He had lost no time in putting his own stamp on the room, personally refinishing the built-in oaken bookshelves in lighter, natural tones and ordering matching furniture from a local carpenter. Evely, his wife, had put the finishing touches on the office by selecting a locally hand-crafted woollen rug and matching curtains to give the room a bright, airy look. The old pastor hadn't said anything the one time he had visited before moving to his retirement home on the other side of the country, but Kingsepp could tell that the changes had upset him. The only thing that Kingsepp had not touched was the row of dark frames housing the portraits of eight former pastors – among whom he expected one day to take his place. But now, the way things were going, he was no longer sure of that. As he glanced over at the far wall, he noticed that the glare from the sun had almost completely washed out the faces of the old pastors, leaving only ghostly outlines of their heads and shoulders. That won't do, he thought, and stirred himself to draw the curtains just enough to block the sun from that area. Much better, he thought as he crossed the room. If only the Russians could be made to go away as easily! On his way back to the armchair, he paused in front of the engraved silver cigarette box on his desk, a going-away present from his first posting in Pärnu. *Should I or shouldn't I? Ah, why not?* he said to himself after briefly hesitating. He had been trying to wean himself from smoking, but under the circumstances another cigarette would make little difference. *What was this call about? Would the major's visit end with his arrest?*

Kingsepp had been living on tenterhooks for the past month, after the overnight arrest and immediate deportation to Siberia of eleven villagers considered to be "anti-Soviet bourgeois elements," a category to which he belonged by virtue of his position. There hadn't been any warning, and the pastor had not known anything about the purge until the following morning when two members of the church council had arrived at the rectory intending to console his wife, and were surprised to find him eating breakfast with his family. "We were sure you would be among the victims, Pastor," Anton Männik, the council chairman, said as Valter Vilde slowly nodded in the background. "There was no announcement, of course, so we're still trying to figure out how many people have been arrested." As the men filled the pastor in on what had happened, they could see that he and his wife were stunned. "They've been taken away already?" the pastor asked as if in a daze. "What about their families? ... Isn't there anything we can do?"

No one spoke. Given what they had heard about arrests in other parts of the country, they knew that the only thing they could do was to pray for the victims. Mr. Männik broke the silence. "I'm sorry to say this, Pastor, but I guess you realize that you are probably their next target. You're going to have to be extra careful from now on."

2

"Oh, Karla," his wife had said. "We have to get away from here." Smiling wanly, the pastor had responded: "Where would we go, Evely?"

The news of the unexpected purge had hit the pastor like a sucker punch to the solar plexus. For the rest of the day he had stumbled around the rectory, unable to talk to anyone. That evening, he rallied slightly to help settle down the children, but instead of getting ready for bed, he then had started to gather some of his things and a couple of blankets and a pillow. "What are you doing, Karla?" Evely had asked. He walked over to Evely's side of the bed, put his arms around her, and gave her a lingering kiss.

"I can't just wait here for the knock on the door," he said. "I'm going to sleep in the hayloft in the barn. That way, I might still have a chance to get away."

"Well, I'm not going to leave the children," Evely said. "You don't have to," Karl responded. "They're not after you. Let's hope I'll be back in the morning."

All that night, Kingsepp had tossed and turned as dire thoughts and dark images, mostly of cattle cars and the frozen wastes of Siberia, kept spiralling through his mind. Just before dawn, he had crept silently back to his bedroom and promptly fallen asleep. When he awoke three hours later, it was to find a rather sad-eyed Evely staring down at him. Neither of them spoke. After a minute or so, Karl got up and started to get dressed. "I don't want to see anyone today," he told Evely. "If someone calls, tell them I'm indisposed. And you can tell Miss Soosaar to take some time off. I need to get away from here for a while; maybe I'll spend the day in the woods."

For three days, the pastor had followed a similar routine, sleeping in the barn and taking long solitary walks in the woods, spending as little time as possible at the rectory, mostly to grab a bite to eat or to help tuck the children into bed. On the fourth morning, Evely came upon him in his office, sitting at his desk smoking and staring vacantly at the portraits of his predecessors on the opposite wall. "You never had to face anything like this, you lucky stiffs," she heard him mutter. It was so sad to see him shrivelling up like this. In her experience, Lutheran pastors tended to be dour, but Karl had always been different, with a sense of

3

humor and a quick and merry laugh. That had been one of his main attractions. She felt tears welling up in her eyes and silently backed away in order not to embarrass him.

Later, when Karl had returned from the woods, she made up her mind to speak to him. "Oh Karla," she said after preparing tea and a ham sandwich for him, "I know it's been hard for you, but don't you think this has gone on long enough? It's not doing anyone any good, least of all you. What am I – and the children – supposed to do while you're off on your own? Have you thought about that? Would it help if I asked Mr. Männik to look in on you? He's always been helpful."

Karl, who had avoided looking at her, raised his eyes to her face before speaking. "I know you're worried, Evely, but I have to work this out for myself. So, no, don't bring in anyone. I can deal with this myself. I just wasn't ready before .... You know how happy we've been ... I had everything I had ever wanted." He stopped and smiled at her. "I couldn't cope with the idea that our life as we've known it, might be over. I didn't know what to do, so I panicked ... but I've realized that there's no easy answer – certainly not dwelling on what's past, and not running away." He took a deep breath before continuing. "I've let you down, you and everyone else. These are dark days, but isn't that what faith is for? At least, that's what I've been preaching on Sundays. So I have to stiffen my backbone and set a good example. I can see that now, and that's how I intend to carry on. I want to be the man I used to think I was."

Evely let out a deep breath, her face relaxing. "You are, Karla, and you always will be. But I too have been thinking," she said, putting her arms around him. "I want us to stick together. That way, we can deal with it, somehow."

"Amen to that," Karl said, drawing her close to him.

Three weeks had gone by since that time, and while the pastor and Evely remained anxious, no one bothered them and life in the rectory had settled back into more or less the old ways. The only change the pastor had made in his ministry was to start writing out his sermons and to deliver them exactly as written. He had noticed that one or two of the local communists had started attending services, obviously hoping to catch him criticizing the Soviet Union, and he didn't want to give them any ammunition by making

4

careless off-the-cuff remarks.

Now the commissar was coming to call. Why? As far as he could tell, he hadn't said anything or done anything to offend the new regime. The pastor had not yet met Commissar Zhukov, but knew of his reputation as a hardliner who everyone said it was not safe to cross. The commissar's assistant and interpreter, however, a burly ethnic Estonian from Russia named Karl Kivisik, remained an enigma to the villagers – always coldly professional and deferential to Zhukov in public, but more sociable when on his own.

The longer he waited for the two men, the more anxious Kingsepp became. *Was their failure to arrest him a month ago an oversight that they now wanted to fix? What else could it be? Unless.... No, surely it couldn't be about the motorcycle he had purchased a year ago to expedite his pastoral visits to the furthest reaches of his widespread parish.*

The problem was that the Russians had confiscated his motorcycle and allocated it to one of the Red Army dispatch riders. A week ago, Vassily, a 22-year-old corporal, had crashed the pastor's motorcycle into a tree on a tricky curve while riding alone late at night. Most villagers wrote it off as a case of drinking and driving, but one of the soldier's comrades, after a quick look at the twisted wreckage, had strongly hinted that the bike's brakes may have been tampered with. Because it was *his* motorcycle, it didn't take long for a rumor to start that the village was home to a "killer priest." The pastor was sure no one in his right mind would pay any heed to such talk, but he knew that rumors of even less substance sometimes led to arrests.

Now, as he stood by the window waiting for the commissar and mulling over that incident, he dismissed the idea as highly unlikely: *If they wanted to arrest me, they'd do it anyway, without needing an excuse.* As he paced back and forth, he searched his memory for anything else he might have said or done that could have provoked the Reds. Nothing came to mind. He tried picking up *The Brothers Karamazov* again, but found he still couldn't concentrate. Despite the open window, he felt hot. Perhaps he should step outside for a minute.

The office, which occupied a separate wing away from the residential part of the rectory, had its own entrance to the

5

carriageway leading up through the park. He had just gone through the outer office, really a waiting room where Miss Soosaar had a small desk, when he heard a car approaching. He stood by the open doorway, watching the black sedan slowly wind its way up the long driveway. It stopped in front of where he stood and two men in civilian clothes got out of the back seat.

"Ah, Pastor, you are very kind to come out to meet us," said the blond, beefier man in Estonian. "Nice place you have here," he said looking around. "Looks big enough for four or five families." The shorter and slimmer dark-haired man, who stood a step ahead of Kivisik, said nothing. Neither of them was smiling. *Hard to tell*, thought Kingsepp. *No soldiers, except a driver... that's a good sign... but they don't look like they're on a social call.*

"*Tere. Mina olen Major Yüri Zhukov,*" the dark-haired man suddenly said in an obviously rehearsed, heavily-accented Estonian as he stepped forward. He didn't offer to shake hands and didn't make any further effort to speak Estonian. He just stood there, staring fixedly at Kingsepp until the pastor said, "Please come in." As they filed into the inner office, Kivisik quickly stepped ahead of Kingsepp and brought the pastor's armchair to the front of his desk to make a small semi-circle with the two visitors' chairs. Kingsepp watched quietly as Zhukov took his time settling into *his* chair. Kivisik meanwhile motioned the pastor to one of the visitors' chairs.

Kingsepp was surprised by how quickly Zhukov got to the point. There was no small talk, just Zhukov making his strange pitch in staccato bursts of Russian. Then, while Kivisik translated, Zhukov would stare at the pastor like a pugilist measuring his opponent's mettle, or more likely, trying to intimidate him. Well, two can play the same game, thought the pastor, and though it took a great effort on his part, he returned Zhukov's stare with a level gaze of his own. It was hard to know what to make of Zhukov's speech, or rather his rant, the pastor thought. It was like something that might have been written by a political satirist, and if the situation had not been so serious, he might have been tempted to laugh.

"There is no place for religion in a progressive society," Zhukov began. "When we have done our work, religion will no longer be necessary. Your people are still at a primitive stage, but with the proper education they can move forward quickly. You're an intelligent man, a university graduate, a silver medalist, so it must pain you to have to make your living by telling lies and catering to old-fashioned prejudices. Now you can speak honestly. The people need to know that religion is a sham, that there is no God; that Marxist-Leninist values are all they need. That would have a big impact, coming from you." With a rather sly look, he added: "We are looking for intelligent Estonians to help us rebuild your country. You were highly recommended by one of your professors in Tartu. If you agree to be our director of religious affairs, you will be based in Tallinn, with your own office and staff. You will be required to travel, so you will have a car and a driver. Also, a nice house, so your wife and children will have everything they need. So what do you say?"

Kingsepp felt his heartbeat quicken as the anger he had been struggling to control rose in his gorge. *Do they think I am a hypocrite? That I can be bought so easily? And who was the idiot professor who recommended me?* He had enough sense, however, to know that it would be dangerous to let his anger show. He struggled for a few moments to find adequate words, and then leaned forward to speak.

"I seem to recall," he began, looking squarely into Zhukov's eyes, "that a long time ago you spent a number of years in prison for being a communist. You could have been released if you had given up those ideas. But you were sincere in your beliefs and refused to change them. And I can see that you still believe in Marxism and Leninism. Well, I'm just like you. I'm no hypocrite. My belief in God and in Jesus Christ is equally sincere. I can't change that even if I wanted to. So I have to refuse your request."

Zhukov said nothing; he just stared back at him for a few moments. "Then your life is going to be a hard one," he finally said in Russian before turning to Kivisik. "This is a waste of time. Let's go."

Kingsepp wasn't sure, but looking back, he thought he had seen something in Kivisik's eyes that was different from the flat, cold stare Zhukov had given him. Whatever it was, he knew things wouldn't end there. Pastors were being arrested in other parts of Estonia, and clearly Zhukov was a dangerous enemy. Come what may, he felt proud that he had been able to overcome his fear and resist that evil man in what he hoped had been a calm and rational manner. But try as he might, he couldn't understand why one of his professors would recommend him to the Reds. He remembered saying that Jesus was a reformer and on the side of the downtrodden, but he had never, ever, even hinted that he had any sympathy for "Capital C" Communism. It must have been a ploy, something Zhukov made up to try to persuade him. Well it didn't work.

As his jumbled thoughts started to sort themselves out, Kingsepp thought that maybe there was a useful insight or two he could glean from the bizarre encounter he had just lived through. For one thing, the rumor of a "killer priest" could not have resonated with Zhukov or he would never have propositioned him about becoming a Red propagandist. More to the point, it struck him that if the communists wanted to eradicate religion by indoctrination and propaganda, it would be a gradual process, which in turn seemed to suggest that the churches would be allowed to remain open, at least for the time being. If that was the case, did it also mean that he was not earmarked for arrest in the near future? For the first time in nearly a month, he slept well that night.

Chapter Two

Karl Kingsepp had come a long way in his thirty-two years. Among all the people who knew him from his childhood, no one would have predicted that one day he would be the pastor of a large and prestigious rural parish. When he was born in 1908, Estonia was a province of Czarist Russia and the Estonians were still the hewers of wood and drawers of water for the Baltic German nobility that governed on behalf of the Russian overlords. If anyone in his family had bothered to look back, all they would have seen was a centuries-old unbroken line of serfs and farm laborers scratching out their subsistence in southeastern Estonia. No one on either side of the family had ever spent more than two winters in primary school. Looking forward, it would have been hard for them to see how anything would change. The foreign occupiers sat at the top of the pecking order and had long since drawn up the ladders after them.

Jaak and Linda, his parents, were hardscrabble tenant farmers on one of the thousand or so *mõisad,* or large rural estates that dotted the country. In addition to providing ground rent, usually a substantial part of his harvest, to the Count von Manteuffel, Jaak's duties included serving as a gamekeeper and forest warden for his landlord. Karl was their third child, with an older brother and sister, but Elena, his sister, had succumbed to some unknown childhood disease at the age of four and Karl had never known her. He had been a difficult child, Karl freely admitted after he had grown to manhood. Six years younger than his brother Aleksander, he had been cosseted by his mother, who was still in pain from the loss of her daughter. She shielded him from his father's stern discipline until even she grew tired of his willfulness and the mischief he caused as the ringleader of the district's *karjapoisid,* the pre-teen boys who spent their summers minding the Count's cattle. If anyone had actually cared to predict his future, it would have been something along the lines of community nuisance, joker or ne'er-do-well.

Karl's attitude began to change after the first time he experienced the vast gulf separating the social classes in Estonia. He had been nine when he and his brother Aleks had gone with their father to the woods behind the Manteuffels' manor to clear away some fallen trees. The Count's family used to go strolling there when they were in residence, which wasn't often because they spent most of their time at another estate in Finland. Servants weren't supposed to go anywhere near the big house unless they were on duty there, but presuming that the Count was still abroad, their father had risked taking a shortcut through the park. To his chagrin, just as they were about to cross a narrow bridge, he saw the elderly Count strolling towards them. Realizing he couldn't avoid an encounter, he quickly reined in the horse and jumped down from the wagon to stand bareheaded at attention, all the while hissing through the side of his mouth at his sons: "Hats off and stand straight. Keep your eyes down and don't speak unless he speaks to you first."

A moment later the Count, preoccupied with whatever great men think about on their country rambles, passed them by silently, as though they didn't exist. Afterwards, as they drove on, their father was unusually silent and avoided looking at them. Aleksander quietly muttered to his brother: "The Count may be a somebody now but his days are numbered." Karl's thoughts, however, moved in another direction; if there were two kinds of people in the world, then he wanted to be on the side that commanded respect.

Even at nine, he knew enough to realize he had been born on the wrong side of the divide, and would find it nearly impossible to cross the chasm. But two years later his horizons expanded when a neighbor loaned him a book about a plucky youth who was able to overcome his humble origins by acquiring an education. Not much later, Karl's eyes were opened even wider by the surprise appearance of an Estonian preacher in the pulpit of their local Lutheran church one Sunday.

Juhan Kapp was only a candidate for ordination and was there for only a two-month trial period, but his effect on Karl was life-changing. In his sermon Pastor Kapp referred to a great need for Estonian pastors now that Estonia had become a Republic, and offered to meet with any boy who might be interested. Karl was intrigued and managed to summon up the courage to talk to the pastor, who turned out to be friendly and very open about the side benefits of a religious vocation. Karl worried that he was not cut out for that kind of work, but he liked the idea of living in a manse almost as big as the manors of some Baltic barons. After thinking it over for a month or two, Karl told his incredulous parents that his dream was to become a Lutheran pastor. Where did he get such grandiose ideas? they asked. Didn't he know that the younger sons of the Baltic German gentry had always had a virtual lock on those positions? The 1918 Declaration of Independence hadn't changed that, they insisted, no matter what that young pastor had said. But Karl knew that his opportunity had come, though there remained a problem: He might have heard God's call, but how was he going to answer it?

He didn't have the faintest idea, but luckily, his mother rose to the occasion. They all knew that Aleksander, a born farmer, would inherit the family farm, and Karl would have to find his own way. His mother, who had seen too many younger sons turn to drink while eking out a miserable bachelor's existence on their older brothers' farms, was only too glad to fall in with Karl's ambition. She saw potential in the fact that Karl had not only learned to read by himself, but was actually reading every book he could get his hands on. He had so impressed his primary school teacher that the young man made a special visit to the farm to encourage Karl's parents to keep him in school beyond the usual two winters. "He's read more books than I have, and I think he even understands them," the teacher told them.

Even so, in the normal course of events, further schooling would have been out of the question. The family farm had only just been bought under a new government land redistribution program and it was proving difficult to manage the mortgage payments, even with the heavy subsidies. Karl's father's immediate reaction had been to say that he had no money to spare for education. But his mother was able to overcome his father's resistance. She never disagreed with his father, but Karl noticed that when she made a "suggestion," his father would sometimes change his mind after a day or two "of reflection." So it didn't come as a complete surprise when

11

his father told him one day that he was thinking of selling a prize bullock, and in that case there would be enough money to start him off in secondary school. He would prefer Karl to become a veterinarian rather than a pastor, his father had said, but they could settle that later. "This is something we can't really afford, but as long as you do your job as a student, son, I will try to support you." Karl took that to mean that if he should ever falter in his studies, he would end up back at the farm shoveling manure. In later years, when he was bleary-eyed from cramming before an exam, he would recall his father's words and run outside to rub his eyes with snow before carrying on.

The final piece of the puzzle was found when his mother persuaded his father to contact his younger half-brother Joosep, a baker in Tartu city. They hadn't spoken in twelve years, but past quarrels were laid aside and Joosep agreed to help. In return for getting up at five every morning to assist with the day's baking, Karl would be provided with room and board. It was an arrangement that worked well for both Karl and his uncle, and one that they kept for all eight years that Karl was in Tartu, first in secondary school at *Treffner's Gümnaasium* and then at Tartu University.

Tartu, he remembered fondly, opened up new vistas for him. One of the prettiest towns in Estonia, it boasted several highly-rated secondary schools and, of course, the country's oldest university, as well as a large number of cultural institutions. It was a lively place offering many kinds of entertainments that Karl had never seen before, and he enjoyed watching the older students in their colorful academic caps amusing themselves in the many cafés and bars or strolling along the picturesque riverside promenades of the *Ema Jõgi* (Ema River). The river itself was often dotted with boats rowed by young men for sport or to take friends or sweethearts to the picnic grounds upstream. Lacking the means to do any of those things, he curbed his envy by convincing himself that by studying hard, he too would one day be like them.

What Karl didn't expect was that those school years would turn him into a different person. Hugo Treffner, the founder and headmaster of Treffner's Secondary School, was a staunch nationalist who encouraged his students to reject foreign customs and to create an indigenous Estonian culture: "If you boys don't take it upon

12

yourselves to do this, I don't know who will." He had a soft spot for veterans of the War of Independence and often hired them as teachers. He also provided full scholarships for the handful of senior boys who had seen action in the 1918-20 war. Karl, who hadn't been particularly patriotic until then, was moved by their example to march with his classmates down the streets of Tartu in counter-demonstrations against Communist rallies. It was his first taste of political activism, and he reveled in it.

Although he had looked forward to moving up to the university, Karl's first impressions of Tartu University were disappointing. Founded in 1632 during the Swedish occupation of Estonia, the university subsequently had become a well-regarded German institution of higher learning. And that, he thought, was the problem. Tartu had remained a privileged bastion of Teutonic culture. Although Estonian had become the official language of the university after Independence, many of the textbooks were in German, and Germanophile professors often denigrated the achievements of Estonian scholars as "good efforts, not yet up to scratch." That kind of academic snobbery, as well as the social snobbery of the more well-off students gradually caused him to re-evaluate his youthful aspiration to join the elite. If, as it seemed, he could never be accepted by them, why bother? Had his plan to rise in the world been a huge mistake, one of those cosmic jokes that gave one hope only to dash it to the ground? After two years, he began to think that university was not for him and that he should leave. But then he thought of what awaited him back home and changed his mind. Rather than drop out, he'd take a leave of absence to fulfill his military service obligations, and keep his academic options open. That, he soon realized, had been an inspired decision, though in some ways a bit like jumping out of the frying pan into the fire. Military life in the cavalry regiment to which he was posted, was just as awful as he had imagined. But freed from the snobbery of some of his professors and classmates, he regained his self-confidence.

His companions in the regiment were mostly farm boys like himself, the kind of people he had always been most comfortable with. Though he never fell completely into their ways, he often joined the lads in the taverns to smoke cigarettes and drink a few tankards of beer. He even managed a short-term relationship with

Edith, a lively and flirtatious shop girl of 21, whom he had met through one of his new companions. She enjoyed teasing him about his visibly thinning hair and a nose she considered too aquiline; he was no beauty, she said with a laugh, though she admitted that his features were pleasant enough. What bothered him most, however, was that she never hid her roving eye. One day, out of the blue, she told him she had a new "friend," an older, more established man. He had enjoyed her company, but all things considered, he wasn't all that sorry to see her go.

Because his companions knew that he had spent two years studying for the ministry, several of them sought his guidance for a variety of personal problems. Karl, who was by nature an outgoing type, not only enjoyed his role of confidante but found that he had a talent for making helpful suggestions. By the time he completed his military service he no longer cared what the social snobs might think of him. It was enough that his mates liked and respected him. He also had a new sense of vocation. He might not enjoy splitting hairs on arcane theological matters, but he became convinced that he had other, perhaps more useful talents.

Going back to the university was no hardship, now that the most pressing of his anxieties had been laid to rest. The transition was made even easier by the reappearance of his youthful mentor Juhan Kapp, now the Rev. Dr. Kapp, after his graduate studies at the University of Heidelberg. Dr. Kapp, it turned out, had been hired to help re-orient the theology department towards a more progressive kind of theology, one that promised to lessen the grip that fusty dogma had so far had on the clergy. For Karl, once again, a career in the ministry became attractive, giving him the impetus he needed to work hard at his studies. He graduated a close second to the gold medal winner.

His professors encouraged him to accept the offer to join the Bishop's staff in Tallinn that was the reward for the top two students, but he chose instead to serve as an assistant pastor in the countryside. Evely Lepik, whom he met and married 18 months after his ordination, was an ideal helpmate. She seemed to share his values and ideas, and was equally keen to start raising a family. When the living in Vändra became vacant in 1935, they both knew that the parish was the place of their dreams. It was a long shot to think that a relatively inexperienced pastor like Karl would be chosen, but it turned out that what they were looking for was a young, energetic pastor, someone exactly like Karl.

Vändra, famous throughout Estonia for its rich history and a whimsical folk song about a bear hunt in its dense forests, was a thriving provincial village of about 3,000. It was also the administrative center for a number of surrounding hamlets and small farming communities that reached far into the countryside. The entire parish had about 6,000 residents, most of whom were members of the church. Karl looked forward to being their pastor.

He was also much taken by the picturesque 18th century white stucco church with its steeply-pitched red roof and square bell tower. Perched at the edge of the village on a small hillside, it faced a substantial village green, at the center of which stood a grey granite obelisk inscribed with the names of the many villagers who had lost their lives in the 1918-20 War of Independence. Knowing that Vändra had been a bellwether community during the national reawakening period in the previous century, he had made a point on his first visit of exploring its well-kept cemetery. Walking through the rows of iron crosses and granite headstones marking the final resting places of the parish's oldest residents, he had paid his respects, with a bowed head and a prayer, every time he found the grave of one of his heroes: people like Johannes Voldemar Jannsen, a pioneering Estonian newspaper editor who wrote the lyrics of the national anthem; his daughter Lydia Koidula, considered by many to be Estonia's finest poet; Carl Robert Jakobson, the editor of Sakala, the most important 19th century nationalist newspaper; Anton Õunapuu, the founder of the Estonian Boy Scouts who was killed in battle during the War of Independence; and Lilli Sumburg, a leading feminist and journalist.

The newly-restored 14-room, two-storey clapboard rectory was another jewel, set in a four-acre park that featured a small stream and numerous gravel paths that wound through extensive flower beds and groves of majestic oaks. The manse and the adjoining 70 hectare church farm were a 20-minute walk from the village, something the pastor greatly appreciated. "It's everything that I had hoped for, and we'll have all the privacy we would ever want," he told his wife.

The rest of the village, however, was somewhat of a disappointment, a hodge-podge of lackluster buildings with little architectural coherence. Still, it had several impressive amenities; a small 10-bed hospital, a co-educational secondary school known as the Vändra *Gümnaasium*, a small residential school for deaf and dumb children, a police detachment with two constables, and a dozen or so shops and businesses on the main thoroughfare, with a few smaller ones sprinkled around the side streets. Farming, however, was the economic engine of the parish, especially dairy farming and flax cultivation for the two linen factories in the area. As they ended their first visit, Karl's wife turned to him and said: "Yes, we can be happy here."

Chapter Three

Pastor Kingsepp had been in his new position for barely a month when he realized that under its surface calm all was not well in the parish. His first inkling of a problem was sparked by a run-in with the local veterinarian whom he had called to attend to a difficult birthing of a calf at the church farm. After the calf had been saved and the vet was starting to leave, the pastor had innocently remarked that he hadn't yet seen the vet at the church and hoped to have that pleasure soon. He was totally unprepared for the elderly man's angry reaction. "The last thing I need is for someone like you to tell me how to lead my life. If you want me to help you again, you'll have to stop interfering in my affairs. Good day!"

"I should have warned you about old Altosaar," Mr. Männik said when the puzzled pastor mentioned the incident to him. "You know that you're only the second Estonian pastor we've had here. All the others were from the German gentry and always supported their class during feudal times. As a result, many of the farming families to this day have a tinge of anti-clericalism, the Altosaars more than most."

"Let me be frank with you, Pastor," Mr. Männik had continued. "We didn't just pick your name out of a hat. It helped that you are a good speaker, but we chose you because you are young and energetic and because you come from the same background as most of our farmers. There's a lot of pastoral work that needs to be done and we're banking on you to do it. The old pastor was a well-meaning man, but maybe a little too old school, if you know what I mean. He was also city-bred and couldn't really relate to our farmers. I wouldn't say that there are that many Taara believers in the parish, but quite a few farmers still perform some of the old rites to get the blessing of the "Mother spirit of the earth," particularly at seeding and harvest times. Or they prefer some of the old cures still being passed on by the old women, instead of seeing a doctor when they are sick. The old pastor had no patience with any of that and was openly scornful of what he considered pre-Christian practices – which as you can imagine offended some of the people. After a while, I think he got tired and just gave up on his pastoral visits. It was all he could do to keep up with the three dozen weddings, 50 funerals, 40 baptisms and the Confirmation classes with 50 teenagers every year. When you have time to look at the Parish Register, you'll see that he also made notations about who took Communion regularly and who never did. He told me once that on that basis, fewer than half of the parish could be considered practising Christians. So, as you can see, you have your work cut out for you."

The pastor took Mr. Männik's words to heart and worked hard to get to know his parishioners, stepping up his pastoral visits and lingering at the dinners the farmers held to celebrate christenings and weddings and to bring closure to funerals. That occasioned another bit of advice from Mr. Männik. "It's nothing personal, but you should know that when the host presses you to stay longer, he doesn't always mean it. What they really want to do is to relax, have a few drinks and gossip about Juhan's carryings on or Lisa's odd behavior, and they don't feel comfortable doing that with you around. So the time to leave is right after the first round of speeches. But make sure that you take Johannes with you when you leave."

"Why is that?" the pastor had asked. Johannes Vares was the church organist, a sixtyish eccentric whose hairstyle and antiquated suits could have been sported by Beethoven. He was a talented musician and an excellent choir master who many years ago had composed a handful of organ pieces that were still highly regarded in church circles.

"I thought he was over it," Mr. Männik said, "but we've started getting complaints again that he's making a nuisance of himself after he's had a few drinks."

The pastor had noticed that Johannes enjoyed a drink, but as he told Mr. Männik, the organist had always behaved correctly at the gatherings they had attended together.

"That doesn't surprise me," Mr. Männik said. "He somehow manages to hold off until after you leave. Then he makes up for the dry spell in a hurry. After that he can't stop himself any more. He

18

starts buttonholing people and talking their ears off. It's always the same story: How his wife left him. How lonely he is. How he can't write music anymore. And if he's talking to a woman or a girl, no matter how old, he starts asking them for a kiss, just one kiss...until the man of the house has to throw him out, sometimes literally."

"I know it's difficult when you're new and you don't know all the people yet," Mr. Männik had said by way of encouragement. "But you'll learn. It took the old pastor nearly ten years before he figured things out." It struck Kingsepp then that he should have had more chats with the old pastor before he moved away to his retirement home. The only bit of advice the old man had given him hadn't seemed particularly relevant at the time: "Some people may really want to talk to you at social occasions," he had said, "but avoid them like the plague, or you'll be stuck for hours trying to explain to someone in his cups what or who exactly is the Holy Ghost."

By the time the Russians arrived in Estonia five years later in 1940, the pastor had won the trust and affection of most of his parishioners. They liked his open-mindedness and the way he didn't talk down to them, and they accepted him as one of their own. Because of the new energy in the congregation, Mr. Männik, the long-time mainstay of the church council, felt he could finally step down as chairman in favor of a younger man. Peeter Kallas, the manager of one of the linen factories, was elected and one of his first actions was to suggest that since there was more than enough work for two men, the council should hire an assistant pastor. Although there was clear support for the proposal, they had not got around to making a decision before the Russians arrived just months later. Then, of course, it was too late.

That became more and more apparent as the Soviet Union consolidated its hold over its tiny neighbor during the summer of 1940. Their purges effectively wiped out the leadership of the country, which they then replaced in rigged elections with Communist candidates. No one in Estonia talked about good times any longer; things could only get worse, they believed. Two weeks after the commissar's visit to Pastor Kingsepp, the shoe finally dropped when the Soviet politburo in Tallinn outlined new policies for land tenure, education and religion.

The draconian measures were clearly intended to pave the way for a new kind of society based on communist ideology. Everyone was affected, including the two-thirds of Estonians who farmed or lived in rural areas, and who so far had been largely left alone. All agricultural properties of more than 30 hectares would be immediately expropriated by the state. Family farms smaller than that were also nationalized but those farmers were allowed to stay on under a system of "perpetual tenure" provided they did not employ any outside labor. Church and municipal lands of any size were to be confiscated and earmarked for conversion to collective farms. Farmers would be assigned quotas for production, a percentage of which was to be turned over to the state at a fixed price.

A second decree was meant to "correct the errors of bourgeois education and religion." Although churches would be allowed to remain open for the time being, all religious instruction and "religious zealotry" would be banned. The projected reforms in education required all schools to follow a prescribed curriculum as soon as the new textbooks were available. In the meantime, teachers who were judged to be "unreliable" would be replaced. Because a number of questions about implementation and schedules were left open, a public meeting would be held the following week at the secondary school, at which time Karl Kivisik would answer questions and explain how the new measures would be carried out locally.

That weekend, however, the parish got a foretaste of what was in store for them. Obviously emboldened by the new Soviet policies, some of the local communists decided to make a fool of the pastor. Their ringleader was "Red Rosa," a tall, powerfully-built washerwoman – "red" as much for her florid cheeks as for her politics – who told her cronies that men who wore "dresses" on Sunday weren't real men. She would prove that, she said, by throwing a sack over his head and checking out what was under his cassock. She would do this after the next service when the pastor was at the church door shaking hands with his congregants. Sure enough, minutes before the final hymn, she arrived with a half-dozen friends who hung around the doors laughing at her lewd jokes while they waited for the pastor to emerge. Kingsepp, approaching the door from the inside, sized up the situation, and without hesitation walked over to Red Rosa and amiably offered his hand in greeting. "I'm glad to see that you have finally decided to come to church," he said loudly. Taken by surprise, Red Rosa just stood there. Obviously rattled, all she could finally do was shake his hand and stammer "Hello, Pastor" before scurrying away, followed by her pack.

When it was time to go to Kivisik's meeting the following week, only three of the seven members of the church council who had agreed to accompany the pastor showed up. "I guess the others are busy," said Mr. Männik. "Or strategically tied up," responded Valter Vilde with his usual caustic wit. "It doesn't matter," said the pastor. "We don't all have to be there." As they walked down the hill towards the secondary school they noticed a platoon of soldiers lounging under the trees at the far end of the athletics field. They also noted that the stream of villagers and farmers making their way to the school thinned out visibly as people turned aside when they became aware of the soldiers.

Only about sixty people were in the school hall when Kivisik called the meeting to order. He was not there to make speeches or to justify the decrees, he said, but would answer any reasonable questions people might have. He had barely finished speaking when the pastor raised his hand to ask why there were soldiers outside. "Is Comrade Kivisik expecting trouble?"

"Not unless you start it," Kivisik responded tartly while glowering at the pastor. "It's normal procedure to keep order, if you really want to know. Anyone else have any real questions?"

After looking around at the silent audience, Kivisik pointed to one of the farmers who had been talking animatedly to his companions a few minutes ago. The man seemed hesitant but nudged by his friends, stood up to complain that the quotas and fixed prices they had been given were not fair and should be adjusted to take into account the "realities of local conditions."

Kivisik gave the man a stony look before responding: "There will be absolutely no changes in the policies and absolutely no special cases." The farmer, who had avoided Kivisik's gaze, shrugged his shoulders and sat down. The pastor seized the opportunity: "About religious instruction..." he began, but was quickly interrupted by Kivisik. "There will be no religious instruction." Kingsepp tried another approach: "But what about ..." Kivisik again cut him off: "Let me make it clear once and for all: No religious instruction of any kind will be tolerated. That means no Confirmation classes and no Religious Studies classes in the high school here. In fact, pastors – that means you – will not be allowed to teach anything in any school of any kind. Is that clear? When Kingsepp stayed standing as though he wanted to ask another question, Kivisik raised his hand to shut him off: "If no one else has any questions, the meeting is over." As he started to walk away from the podium, he paused to again address the pastor. "You should be grateful your church is still open. I wouldn't push my luck, if I were you."

"Well, I don't call that much of a meeting," the pastor said to Peeter Kallas as they filed out. "I think we need to hold our own meeting to decide what to do now. They're allowing the church to stay open for the time being, but for how long? You heard Kivisik say that we can no longer hold Confirmation classes. To me that's a key issue. Where will our future generations of parishioners come from?"

The following day, on his way to the church for the meeting, the pastor was waylaid by Jaan Koppel, a council member who owned a small clothing shop on the main street. "I wanted to speak to you alone," said Koppel, who had not attended Kivisik's meeting. "I'm worried by the new policies and how you might be planning to re-act. As a businessman, I can't afford to be involved in anything that goes against the new laws." He paused to look expectantly at the pastor.

"Well, I can't lie to you..." the pastor managed to get out before he was cut off by Koppel. "I don't want to hear anything more. This way I'll be able to say I don't know anything about whatever you are up to. I'm sorry it has come to this, but I can't stay on the council any longer. Please give my regrets to the others."

The others were already at the sacristy when the pastor arrived and were disappointed, though not surprised, to hear about Koppel's resignation. "I can't blame him," Peeter Kallas, the chairman said. "Even though the communists claim they'll achieve their goal by evolution, we've seen that they're quite ready to use force to get their way. We're all vulnerable, and I wouldn't be honest if I didn't tell you that I've had a few second thoughts myself...."

"This is serious, but let's not panic," the pastor interjected. "I think I know why I wasn't arrested last month. I didn't tell you this before, but Zhukov came to see me a couple of weeks ago to ask me to leave the church to run some kind of anti-religious propaganda bureau. I turned him down, of course. But it's clear that their plan is to subvert our youth to their way of thinking. The rest of us, the older parishioners, don't really matter. As far as they're concerned, we'll die out anyway. Their real target is the youth. That's why banning Confirmation classes is so serious." He paused for a few moments to emphasize his next remark. "But since they are not planning to close the churches for the time being, we have some breathing space to figure out how to deal with that situation."

"So what can we do?" Toomas Rebane asked.

"I'm not sure how or where," the pastor responded, "but what I want to do is to organize Confirmation classes without the Reds finding out."

"I'd be in favor of that, if we can figure out how to do it," said Valter Vilde, owner of one of the large farms that had been confiscated. "We're losing our land; do we also have to lose our religion? And it's not only our religion; the church also nourishes our culture, what makes us Estonians. Surely we owe that to our children."

"I understand your point," Adam Lootus said. "But Jaan Koppel is right; some of us still have something to lose, and we can't all hide in the woods."

"Everybody doesn't have to be involved," the pastor quickly interjected. "We all have different situations and our own ways of looking at things, so anything we decide has to be on a voluntary basis."

Mr. Männik, who had been listening carefully, now spoke up. "I'm in favor of the pastor's idea, but I don't want to rush into anything we might regret. I think we should look into this matter a little longer and approach it very carefully, if we don't want to end up in the *Gulag* – along with the young people we're trying to help. My boys know a lot of our youths. I suggest we wait until they can sound some of them out to see if this kind of thing is feasible." Seeing all the nods around the table, the pastor also nodded. "Let's leave it at that for now."

On his way home, the pastor fell in step beside Toomas Rebane who had taken the same route. "We wouldn't have to worry about these things so much if all our young people were like the Männik twins," the pastor said, adding after a pause: "Mr. Männik should have had more children." Toomas Rebane looked surprised. "I guess you don't know that they aren't really his sons."

"No, I didn't know that," the pastor said. "Mind you, I sometimes did wonder how a small man like him could have two such giants for sons. Acorns usually don't fall that far from the tree."

"I suppose I should tell you the story," Rebane said. "It may come up again and I wouldn't want you to put your foot in it, especially since it doesn't reflect all that well on some people." Before continuing, Rebane looked up at the pastor, who nodded.

"Anton Männik was an old bachelor when he got married," Rebane began, "and was a newlywed when the War of Independence broke out. Despite that, he never hesitated, but answered the call for volunteers right away. He was severely wounded in a skirmish against the White Russian forces and had to spend nearly a year in hospital before being discharged."

"I thought he might be a war hero. So that's how he got his limp," the pastor said. "I often meant to ask him, but I didn't want to be intrusive. I figured he'd tell me if he wanted me to know."

"Oh, I don't think so, not unless you asked him directly," Rebane said, before continuing his tale.

"Meanwhile, while Anton was off at war, his much younger wife apparently had an affair with another soldier, a former childhood friend, and became pregnant. He was a big, strong good-looking fellow but had no sense of honor. As soon as he found out she was pregnant, he left her and never came back. We heard later that he had been killed in some battle," Rebane said. "Anyway, Anton never knew anything about that. When he came home from the hospital, he found his wife was pregnant and just about ready to give birth. He knew the child couldn't be his, but he still loved his wife and promised her he would look after it. He even said he could understand what she must have been feeling after he went off to the war, and that he forgave her."

"Merike was actually a nice person and I think she did love him in her own way. So you can understand how relieved she must have been... but I guess God didn't forgive her, because she had a really long labor and a hard birth. The second twin had to be helped out with forceps, and there was a lot of bleeding that the doctors couldn't stop. They did what they could, but she didn't survive."

"Anton was devastated. He really did love her despite everything. He had a nursemaid at first, but he brought those two boys up all by himself and loved them like they were his own. Every year on Merike's birthday, they all went together to her grave, and as you know, he still has you say a prayer for her every year. The boys never even knew he wasn't their real father until they were grown up. We all told Anton not to do it. 'What they don't know can't hurt them,' we said. 'Why spoil things?' But you know him well enough by now to know that's not the kind of man he is. He said they have a right to know, and he did tell them on their 21st birthday."

"I guess we shouldn't have been surprised, but nothing changed after he told them. I asked Heiki once whether it was strange to suddenly find out they had another father. And you know what he told me? He said they didn't have another father. Anton was the only father he and Andres had ever had. The fact that some stranger had provided a bit of sperm to get them started did not mean he was their father."

"Anyway, don't let Anton know I told you any of this. He doesn't like to talk about it and we've always respected his wishes. He's the best man I've ever known; without him the parish might have fallen apart years ago."

"I couldn't agree with you more," said the pastor. "Thank you for telling me this, and don't worry, I won't say a word."

Chapter Four

Two days after Kivisik's non-meeting, Pastor Kingsepp received an order addressing what was referred to as an "administrative oversight." Pastors, teachers and other "bourgeois parasites" were henceforth to be included in public work assignments, usually involving the repair of local roads and bridges. His first job would be to haul a pile of logs from the village to a railway station twelve kilometers away before the end of the week. The pastor had been raised on a farm, so the prospect of physical work didn't frighten him. Sometimes, just for his own pleasure and for the exercise in it, he used to hitch up a horse and help with the plowing or harvesting on the church farm. But when he went to do his assigned task, he saw that completing the job within the time limit would be beyond the power of any one man. *So, that's how it was going to be,* he thought. They would fill his time with physical labor to keep him from performing his pastoral duties. Or worse, they wanted him to fail, so that they would have another excuse for getting rid of him. Well, he would do his best, so that at least they couldn't charge him with resisting orders. But first he needed to borrow a more suitable team of horses from Mr. Männik. Although the elderly farmer had resigned from the chairmanship of the church council, he had maintained a fatherly eye on the pastor and was always ready to help in any way he could. Despite the disparity in their ages, he had asked the pastor to call him by his first name, though he himself always addressed Karl as "Pastor." Kingsepp, who had been brought up to respect his elders, could never bring himself to do that. "Mr. Männik" sounded just right to him, even if he did call everyone else on the council by his first name.

When the pastor went to Mr. Männik's farm to seek help that evening, he found the farmer alone in his kitchen drinking a mug of tea. "You don't look too happy, Pastor. I'll get you a cup and then you can tell me your troubles. I bet it has something to do with those damn Ruskies."

"What else could it be?" the pastor answered. "If it wasn't for them, we wouldn't have any troubles."

After the pastor had outlined his problem, the feisty old widower smiled and joked that a better use of the horses would be to pull down the commissar's privy. "But don't worry," he said. "I'll get my boys to help. The job's as good as done."

Two weeks later, the pastor was assigned another nearly impossible task – to haul several tons of gravel to a road repair site many kilometers distant. Mr. Männik again came to his rescue with his team and his sons, so again the task was completed expeditiously.

Two more tasks were assigned, with similar results, but then the new regime seemed to run out of make-work jobs, for nothing more was heard from them for several weeks.

Still, the pastor was not easy in his mind. He doubted very much that they would leave him alone. In their "workers' paradise" there was no place for people like him, and Zhukov had promised him a "hard life." Whenever his time was up, he knew it would come with a midnight knock at his door.

"I think you are right to be worried," Mr. Männik told the pastor one evening after they had discussed matters over a cup of tea. "The commissar may not be after you right now, but he certainly won't lift a finger to help if anyone wants to take matters into his own hands. And as we've seen, the way things are escalating that's always a possibility. It might be a good idea to vary your routine occasionally... maybe sleep over at some of the outlying farmhouses from time to time."

"I can't do that," the pastor answered. "When the first purges happened, I wanted to flee from here, but I caught myself in time, and I resolved then that I would never let them run me to ground. I intend to carry on in my job the best I can for as long as I can."

"I admire your spirit, Pastor," Mr. Männik said, "but this is not the time to take chances. It's not cowardly to be prudent, you know. I wouldn't be walking around with a limp now if I had listened to that advice when I was in the war. We want you to stay alive. You're much more use to the parish that way."

"You may be right," Kingsepp said. "What about if I try that out for a couple of weeks to see how it goes?"

The next day, he told Evely that because he would be at home only on random evenings for the next few weeks, she should take their two children on an extended visit to her family in Viljandi. Even though Evely wasn't particularly close to her parents, especially her father, she agreed that would be the best way to keep the children out of harm's way. Her two brothers, Mati and Mark, and Mark's wife Hilda, a former classmate whose two daughters were not much older than Evely's own children, would help keep her mind off events in the parish.

Chapter Five

A week later, the pastor had to go for a Christening at the Soovere family's small farm some 20 kilometers up in the wilder northern part of the parish. Getting away from the village these days was a pleasure, and he was fond of Enn Soovere, who reminded him more than a little of the companions of his youth. Like them, Enn never had much to say, but he was a jovial, kind-hearted man who could always be counted on to do the right thing. And Jutta Soovere, an accomplished cook, would have prepared a special dinner to celebrate the birth of her first son.

After the Christening, when the two dozen neighbors and relatives had sat down around the trestle tables in the farmyard, Kingsepp's final duty before relaxing was to say grace and extend the congratulations and best wishes of the congregation to one-month-old Tarmo and his parents. The proud father then stood, raised his tumbler of homemade vodka, and almost shouted a "Prosit" as he pointed at the array of dishes on the table. "I know that this is what we've all been waiting for, so everybody help yourselves. There's plenty more." The food was every bit as good as expected, and prompted by the host, the pastor happily accepted second helpings of everything, all the while chatting with the guests sitting closest to him. No one seemed particularly eager to make a speech – which suited him just fine. All too often, the speeches at these events, he had found, rambled on and on through various maudlin twists and turns with no end in sight. But then, an hour or so later, just as he was about to get up to take his leave, a distant cousin from outside the district clinked his spoon against his glass and called for order. "If you will allow me, I would like to say a few words to welcome the new addition to Enn and Jutta's family. In these troubled times, it is a brave thing to bring a child into this world, but knowing Enn and Jutta like I do, I have to say ...."

Having heard dozens of such speeches, the pastor knew they

were in for the long haul. He was only half listening to a nearly year-by-year account of Enn and Jutta's childhood, courtship and marriage, when the speech suddenly turned into a diatribe against the communists who, the cousin vehemently declared, were a *saatana nuhtlus,* or the devil's scourge, and deserved to be eradicated. Everyone's ears perked up, and the guests soon began to vent their own bottled up anger. It was rare to hear people talking so candidly, and the pastor, who got caught up in listening to them, hardly noticed how the time was slipping away. So it was considerably later than he had planned when he saddled up and started for home on what he expected would be a pleasant canter in the late afternoon sun.

Half way to the village, he was surprised to see coming towards him on the usually deserted road a motorcycle carrying two Russian soldiers. Neither of the men seemed to pay any attention to him, and he ignored them, but shortly after they had passed he heard an angry shout that sounded something like "killer priest," followed by a rapid shifting of gears and the revving of the bike's engine.

"Oh, damn," the pastor said under his breath and kicked his horse into a gallop without turning his head to confirm what he had already sensed. He had a good head start, but knew that there was no way he could outrun the motorcycle, even though he was on his favorite horse Tasuja ("Avenger"), the frisky mare that had been bred and raised by his father as an ordination present for him. His only hope would be to get into the woods before they were able to cut him off, but he knew that that would be touch-and-go on this densely wooded, uninhabited stretch of road.

They were rapidly gaining on him and soon were close enough to shoot if they had wanted to kill him, but no shots rang out as he leaned lower and pushed Tasuja to go even faster. He was thankful now for the year of military service he had spent in a cavalry regiment; without that experience, he would surely have fallen off by now.

He deliberately kept riding down the middle of the road where the footing was most secure and he would be less likely to be nudged into the deep ditches on either side. Soon the motorcyclists were almost directly behind him, but they made no effort to pass him on the narrow road.

Karl risked a quick glance behind and saw the pillion rider remove his belt and start swinging at the horse's rump. They couldn't get close enough to do much damage, but one or two of the blows found their mark. Tasuja, however, didn't falter. Even at a slightly wider spot, where the motorcycle could have easily cut in front of the pastor, they held back. They were toying with him, the pastor thought, not necessarily trying to kill him, though if he fell off that would be the likely result.

He knew he was getting close to a narrow trail through the woods leading to an old logging camp. It was hidden by trees and was at a sharp angle to the road, so it could easily be missed. But it was probably his only hope to get away from the motorcyclists before his horse threw him. He would have to make the dangerous turn at a gallop, but he thought Tasuja could probably handle that. Anyway, it was a risk he would have to take.

Just as they were approaching the trail, the motorcyclists seemed to be pulling abreast of him, as though they had tired of the game they were playing, and were about to do something more serious. It was now or never, he thought, and pulled sharply on the reins, causing Tasuja to skid and half stumble as she entered the sharp turn. But she hung on and recovered to pound off down the trail while the motorcycle kept going at full speed past him on the road.

He knew he was safe now, that there was no way they could follow him through the maze of paths that he knew like the back of his hand. He stopped to listen, but there was no sound of pursuit, so saying a quick prayer of thanks, he patted his heavily lathered horse and trotted through the woods to the Männik's farm. Best not to go to his own house right now, he thought.

Mr. Männik was relieved to see him. "I have to say I was worried about you after the news I heard this afternoon. You wouldn't have known this, but Vassily, the fellow who fell off your bike, died last night without regaining consciousness. So I'm not surprised by what you just told me. Those two hotheads were probably friends of his who took advantage of a chance encounter to try to avenge him. I don't think they'll pursue the matter when they cool off, but don't let your guard down, just in case. If

33

anything, I would advise you to move around the farms even more than you've been doing. You can sleep here tonight for a start."

Chapter Six

When the new regime forbade the use of hired help, the Kingsepps had been obliged to send away the manse's housekeeper, Reet Sillaots, and her husband, Hannes, their gardener and general factotum. The Pindams, who looked after the model dairy run by the church, also had to leave when they were co-opted to manage a collective farm in another district. Only Jukku Tamm, their taciturn tenant farmer, who had been told that ten hectares of the church farm were now his, had been permitted to stay in his little cottage a half-kilometer from the manse.

Evely, with two young children, sorely missed Reet's's helping hand in the rambling 14-room rectory, so she was happy enough to continue staying with her family in Viljandi. Her mother, who suffered badly from arthritis, was not able to help very much with minding the children, but Auntie Minna, her mother's childless younger sister, whom she called Tädi (aunt), was only too glad to help. She was very fond of the children and was delighted to look after them. Her willingness to help and her many years of experience as a parlor maid for the Baltic German gentry helped to make Evely's life considerably easier. Very quickly, even though Evely had not known her aunt very well, a warm and loving relationship had developed between them.

Auntie Minna had made a late-life marriage to Jüri Reimann, who like her had been employed for more than 30 years at Count von Mentzenkampf's *Taevavärav Mõisa* (Heaven's Gate Manor) near Suure-Jaani, she as a housemaid, he as a gardener. While their paths often crossed, it couldn't be said that they knew each other very well. He was twelve years older than she was, a quiet man who mostly kept to himself. Unbeknownst to anyone, he had saved enough money to buy a small farm to which he planned to retire. *Metsa Talu*, (Forest Farm) was somewhat rundown, and more than half of its 24 hectares were uncleared forest or undrained bog; but it had been all he could afford and he had worked hard to make the farmhouse habitable and to plant a spectacular flower garden.

One day, out of the blue and without any attempt at courtship, he had proposed to Minna, saying that he wanted to share his retirement and his farm with her. That was eight years ago, when she was 54 and resigned to the life of an old maid. The proposal, she thought, was a much better alternative than eventually moving in with Evely's mother and father. To everyone's surprise, the marriage between the elderly wallflowers had been a success, though of short duration. Only six years later, Jüri, a heavy smoker, had been diagnosed with terminal lung cancer.

Having no family of his own, Jüri told Minna that the farm should be passed on to her family, even insisting that they formally adopt one of her sister's children, who would then be his legal heir. Evely had been suggested by her parents, since neither of her city-bred brothers was interested in becoming a farmer. Mark, the oldest, was a career soldier; Mati, a late-life addition to the family, was still a teenager but had already set his heart on a career as a sports coach or gym teacher.

Evely wasn't married at that time and at 26, at least in some eyes, had already been relegated to spinsterhood. Her father Kalle, who liked to think of himself as a ladies' man, couldn't understand why. "A good-looking girl like that? I shouldn't have sent her to secondary school," he began to tell people. "Men don't want women to be smarter than them." Having the prospect of a farm in the future might help her get off the shelf, he reasoned, so he was very much in favor of Jüri's idea. As it turned out, the farm played no role at all in her marriage to Karl Kingsepp, who a few years later did not feel threatened by the prospect of an educated wife.

Karl's clock had also been ticking. A bachelor pastor would have a hard time finding a good parish, he was warned. That was brought home to him very plainly at his previous posting as an assistant pastor in Pärnu. One day, Pastor Valdo Kuusk, the senior pastor, had surprised him by asking what he thought of a certain young lady in the parish.

"She seems very nice," he had said somewhat guardedly. "Maybe she could be more regular in attending services, but that seems to have improved lately. Why do you ask?"

The older pastor kept silent for a moment or two, as though he wasn't sure how, or even whether, to continue. With a slight shrug, he decided to forge ahead.

"Well, do you know that she has told her friends that she is going to marry you before the end of the summer?"

Kingsepp was flabbergasted. "No, I didn't know that. It's not only a complete surprise to me; it's ridiculous. Surely you don't believe I would ...." He stopped suddenly. "Really, I have no idea why she would say that."

"Well, that's what my wife heard from Tiiu's mother," Kuusk continued. "Apparently, you have been staring at her during services and she sees that as meaning it is only a matter of time before you go to see her parents. Is there any truth in that?"

Kingsepp's heart fell. He had no idea that anyone had noticed. For a few months now he had caught himself staring at some of the younger women in the parish, especially Tiiu, who, it had to be said, was a looker. Whenever he had realized he was staring, he tried to look away before he was noticed. Obviously he had not succeeded. "I guess I might have looked at her a few times," he said blushing. "But I didn't mean anything by that."

Pastor Kuusk chuckled. "I'm glad to hear that's all it is. Don't worry, most of us go through a looking phase when we're single, but you can't be too obvious about it. Anyway, it seems it might be time for you to seriously think about getting married...." He stopped abruptly as Kingsepp made a choking sound. "No, no, not Tiiu; I don't think she would make a good pastor's wife."

Kingsepp hadn't realized how tense he had become until he felt himself relax; his natural color returned and his breathing became more normal. Pastor Kuusk, too, seemed relieved. "Well, that's that, but you should give some thought to what I said," Pastor Kuusk said as he left the rectory office smiling.

It wasn't long after that, that he had met Evely at a choir festival in the parish. He was a lucky man, he thought. Even after five years of marriage, they liked to stroll hand in hand around the grounds of the manse while chatting amiably. "Inge," a black and white border collie half-breed that came with the church farm, quickly became Evely's pet and trotted after them on their walks. After the birth of the children, they still continued the walks, often with one of them pushing a perambulator.

After Juri Reimann's death, just before the Russians arrived, Evely became the legal owner of the Metsa Talu farm, but Auntie Minna remained in residence. When the communists changed the land tenure laws, Karl and Evely began to take more interest in the farm. Falling below the 30-hectare limit for permissible private holdings and with half of the acreage thickly wooded or marshy, it could be a useful refuge, a place where they might even be able to carry on their lives away from Red scrutiny, if that ever became necessary. Before long, Evely found herself spending more time with her aunt in Suure-Jaani than at her parents' home in Viljandi. It was clear to them both that Tädi was becoming an integral part of her adopted daughter's household and would move back to the manse with Evely when they felt less threatened by the Reds.

Chapter Seven

When a week had gone by without any follow-up to the harrowing motorcycle chase, the pastor felt able to again spend odd days at the manse in order to have access to his books. Left to his own devices, Kingsepp, who was a hopeless cook, usually made do with a sliced pork sandwich and a glass of buttermilk. On his first night back, because there was a church council meeting, he had quickly washed his one plate and glass and was sitting at the kitchen table smoking and reading while he waited for Mr. Männik to drop by. It had become their custom to stroll to the church together while running through the evening's agenda. Because most villagers avoided the shadowy stretch of road that passed the cemetery, it was always a peaceful and pleasant walk during which they could chat leisurely while enjoying the evening air.

That evening, however, there was little time for chit-chat, as the meeting had a full agenda and Mr. Männik wanted to brief the Pastor on a number of items. First of all, he said, his sons had been unable to make much headway with the plans for a secret Confirmation class. "It seems like a lot of the boys are more interested in clandestine resistance groups like the *metsavennad* (forest brothers) or even the Boy Scouts. My sons also have to be very careful whom they talk to, so it's slow going, but they'll keep trying." Next, he said, Peeter Kallas, the new chairman, might not be at the meeting. "Like he told us at the last meeting, as the manager of the linen factory, he is under a lot of pressure from the Reds. He was supposed to meet with Kivisik this afternoon, so that doesn't bode well. Also, Juhan Lind is at it again. This time he and his friends want us to stop ringing our church bells."

The pastor smiled wryly. Lind was the man who had shown up in church one week and had sat in a central pew ostentatiously reading a newspaper to show his disdain for religion. Some of the parishioners were offended and had wanted to throw him out, but the pastor had convinced them to ignore Lind. "He's not a well man," he had said, "but he's harmless."

"I'll try to talk to Lind," he now said. "Maybe he'll be satisfied if we give him a small victory – say we ring the bells more quietly and for shorter periods of time – but I don't hold out much hope. If he goes to the commissar, we'll probably have no choice but to silence the bells."

"One last thing," Mr. Männik said. "I heard from Andres, who… well, it doesn't matter where I heard it. What's important is this: They're going to start taking over the confiscated farms next week. I think they held off until after the harvest so they could take the crops as well. Anyway, I'm pretty sure the church farm will be the first on their list. I know how much you depend on the harvest, so I started thinking about that and I had an idea. We could salvage at least a part of it if we act quickly…and by that I mean tonight. The only problem is where to put everything. It can't be anywhere near here."

"I've been thinking along those lines myself," the pastor said, "and I know what we can do. You know that farm of my wife's that I told you about in Suure-Jaani. It's just far enough away to be safe, but not too far, about 20 kilometers. It's somewhat run-down, but there's a new roof on the barn. If you're serious about helping, we could start moving things tonight."

"Absolutely," Mr. Männik said. "Right after the meeting. It will be dark enough by then."

The two men finished the walk to the church in silence. As usual, they were the first to arrive, but within minutes, others trickled in, leaving only Peeter Kallas and two new members to come. As they sat around the table making small talk and smoking, the pastor kept glancing at the wall clock, whose ticking for the first time struck him as irritatingly loud. After 15 minutes, when it became apparent the others were not coming, he suggested that Mr. Männik chair the meeting.

"I'm afraid that most of what we have to discuss tonight, as usual these days, has to do with the communists," Mr. Männik said. "But why don't we first listen to the pastor's report on the state of the parish. I'm sure he'll find something to start us off on a positive note."

Sure enough, the pastor's first words were meant to be encouraging. "It's not easy, but the parish is learning how to live under Communism. For one thing, church attendance remains high, even better than before. I interpret that as a kind of healthy passive resistance, if I may call it that. Also up is the number of people taking Holy Communion. And the number of Christenings and weddings has also increased. The only downside is that the number of funerals is up slightly too."

"I'm not surprised," Valter Vilde chimed in, "Who would want to live under the Reds?"

"By the way, Pastor," Toomas Rebane, a keen patriot, said. "You mentioned passive resistance. That's all we seem to be doing. But I thought you were looking into ways to..."

"Thank you, Toomas," Mr. Männik quickly interjected. "I think we all know that there are things it is best not to talk about these days. When the time is ripe, all will be revealed."

"I'd like to say something about that," the pastor said. "It's a matter of choosing our opportunities. Open defiance is impossible, but our people are nonetheless sending a message to the Communists by attending church in these numbers. We're not giving up the struggle, just playing it smart, like the forest brothers. They're not confronting the Reds; they're holding themselves ready for the right moment."

"Well spoken, Pastor," Mr. Männik said, to a chorus of "Hear, Hear" and "Amen."

"One more thing," the pastor said, holding up his hand to quiet them. "I want to say that I'm particularly proud of our youths. Most of them are solidly against the new regime, but they're also holding themselves in check. You know that when Zhukov sent his thugs to pull down our Independence War monument, the boys from the secondary school went there later that night and gathered up all the pieces and hid them somewhere in the woods. They know that Estonia will be free again one day and then they'll be ready to rebuild the monument. That's the way we should all think and act."

"My son was one of them," Toomas Rebane said proudly.

"You raised him well, Toomas," Mr. Männik said. "But be careful where you say that.... Let's move on. We have more items we need to cover. So next: You all know that the church farm has been confiscated. That's going to leave the pastor's family short of food.

41

We're hoping to save some of the current crop, but it won't be enough to last the winter. So I'm proposing that we ask the farmers among us to put aside anything we can spare for the pastor's family..."

"Just a minute, Anton," Valter Vilde interrupted. "If I understand you correctly, you want the farmers to help the pastor? I'm all for that, of course," he said looking at the pastor and then at Mr. Männik, "but what about the villagers? Why does it always have to be the farmers who make the sacrifices? Some of us are losing our farms. Why can't the villagers pitch in, too?"

Mr. Männik sighed. "Of course, Valter. I'm sorry I misspoke myself. I meant to say that all the members of the congregation should be asked to help. Can we agree on that?" They all nodded, Vilde more energetically than the others.

"Speaking of everyone, why isn't Peeter here?" Jüri Laansoo, asked, looking worried. "He's never been late before. And where are Andrus and Siiman?"

"I think Zhukov may have got to Peeter," Hans Oder, the treasurer, said. "I know he's been targeting the younger men, trying to frighten them with his 'You're either for us or against us' threats. I don't want to speak for him, but I know Peeter has been worried for some time. He's already a marked man as a manager, so he's been worried that staying on as the chairman of the council might be the straw that breaks his back."

The pastor nodded. Peeter Kallas was an exceptional administrator and a committed Christian, exactly the kind of man the church needed – and the communists abhorred.

He had also seen in Peeter, who was near his own age, the possibility of a type of friendship he had not had since his university days. His bosom pal then had been Hjalmar Herne, a Swedish-Estonian transfer student, whom he had met in one of his classes after returning from his military service break. They shared a mutual disdain for the fundamentalist views of their professor, and discovered a common enthusiasm for chess and serious literature. They also enjoyed studying together and often had animated conversations while taking long walks along the Ema River. But Hjalmar had moved back to Sweden after graduation and the letters they still exchanged only slightly assuaged his need for a kindred spirit, especially after Evely found her time largely taken up by the children. Losing Peeter from the council would be a major disappointment.

"If he's really gone, we need to deal with that," Kingsepp told his quietly waiting council. "Andrus and Siiman will be missed, but I think we can manage without them for the time being. The chairman's position, however, is different. There are many things to organize that require an experienced hand. I hope he doesn't, but if Peeter really does resign," Kingsepp said looking at Mr. Männik, "would you consider coming back as chairman?"

Mr. Männik didn't hesitate. "If all the council members agree, I would. The Reds won't care about an old fellow with a limp like me. It's the youngsters they want to scare away." As he was speaking they heard the sound of the outer church door opening. "*Kurat*, if that's the Reds, we better go out the back way," one of the startled members said. "No we won't," the pastor said. "At least I won't. If they're coming to arrest us, let them do their worst. We can show them what Christians are made of."

"The pastor is right," said Mr. Männik. "If anyone wants to go they should do that now, but I'm going to stay here." In fact, he said, picking up a heavy brass candlestick from the shelf behind him, "I'm going out there now in case it's just one of those commie vandals looking to cause trouble."

He hadn't taken more than two steps past the sacristy door into the church, when he turned and shouted. "Don't go anyone. It's Peeter and Siiman."

The pastor felt a surge of happiness to see the two men, but Peeter's first words were not reassuring. "I'm sorry I didn't come sooner, but Siiman and I had to think things through. We've come to explain our decision in person...."

"So you are resigning," anticipated Mr. Männik.

"Yes, we are, and Andrus also. He decided not to come, so we're also speaking for him," Peeter said. "I know it may seem cowardly, but we've been seriously warned today. All three of us have young families and we feel our first obligation is to them. It's only temporary, depending on how things go. As soon as it quiets down, we would like to come back, but we don't feel it is safe to be on the council at this time. They're watching us, they said, so even coming

here tonight could be a problem. That's why we have to go now.
Forgive us, please."

Chapter Eight

After the disappointing outcome of the meeting, the saddened pastor returned to the rectory to prepare for the night's farm-moving. As he was changing into his work clothes, it suddenly struck him that Jukku Tamm was still in his cottage on the church farm, making it impossible to move anything without being seen or heard. Could Jukku be trusted? Six months ago, the pastor would have had no qualms about Jukku's reliability, but now he wasn't so sure.

Like the pastor, Jukku came from a long line of tenant farmers, all of whom had been workers on the large Baltic German estates that used to own virtually all of the productive agricultural land in Estonia. Only after the establishment of the Republic had land reform laws made it easier for Estonians to own their own small family farms. Nevertheless, old habits and dependencies persisted and a significant tenant farmer class still existed in the countryside – people like Jukku who seemed to have little ambition for anything other than to keep body and soul together with work and the occasional bottle of vodka.

The previous pastor had been city-raised and was not interested in the farm as long as it provided food for his table and didn't run a deficit. Kingsepp, a farmer's son, loved the smell of freshly-plowed soil and the way the small bright green seedlings turned into shimmering seas of darker green and gold. He had seen immediately that the church farm, on prime agricultural land, was not as productive as it could be. In that respect, he was like his father, he thought; he hated to see things done in half-measures.

After observing the workings of the farm for a few weeks, he had cautiously suggested that Jukku start to do things a little differently, more in line with the modern practices advocated by the ministry of agriculture. He had sent away for pamphlets and bought new varieties of seeds, but to little avail. Jukku was not one to abandon his accustomed routines and he left the unread pamphlets lying around the barn. Under constant prompting, however, he had grudgingly taken up a few of the suggestions. Once, the pastor had been told, Jukku had been overheard in the tavern boasting about how *his* new methods had increased crop yields.

Then the Reds arrived, and everything changed again. After they took over all farms of more than 30 hectares, they forbade the remaining small, family farms to use hired laborers. This was to be a first step towards a classless society, the farmers were told. Tenant farmers, like Jukku, were also told that they now had the right to claim ten hectares of their former landlord's land as their own.

The pastor knew that the Reds' propaganda would reverberate well with landless tenant farmers, but he now wished he had made more of an effort to sound out Jukku's views. They had had only one short discussion the time Jukku had asked him whether Christ could have been a Communist. Maybe it wasn't so bad, Jukku had said, if the land was used for everyone's benefit, not just the rich people.

The pastor had been caught off guard, but he agreed that Christ's teachings had been especially mindful of the wretched and the poor of this earth. However, he quickly added, there was a big difference. The Reds used force to implement their ideas, and were imprisoning or killing people who disagreed with them. Such a bad start, he said, could not produce a good result. He was certain Christ would not have approved.

Jukku had only smiled, as though that was what he had expected the pastor to say, and had stopped asking questions. When Jukku started missing Sunday services, Kingsepp realized he had never really taken the trouble to get to know this man who had worked for him. He wanted to rectify that but didn't quite know how, since Jukku, who now was his own boss, seemed to be avoiding him.

As these thoughts rolled through his mind, he reluctantly decided that they couldn't afford to take a chance. If even a hint of what they were doing got back to the Reds, he and the Männiks would surely end up in the *Gulag*.

"You're early," Mr. Männik, who was still eating supper, said when the pastor arrived at his neighbor's farm. "I thought we had agreed to go at midnight. My boys are still out there keeping an eye on the sexton's lad. As you know, of course, he's the fellow watching you. He's pretty transparent, actually. He always follows the same routine, hanging around the churchyard and the manse, ending up at the tavern every night around ten. He's always home by midnight and then you never get another peep out of him. That's when we'll go."

The pastor had never thought Randar was much of a threat; he was a rather morose and uncommunicative 30-year-old, who seemed to spend much of his time, when not helping his father dig graves, hunched over a beer mug. Recently he had noticed him spending more time than usual loitering around the church properties. The rumor that he had joined the Communist Party seemed to be confirmed when he was seen helping the Soviet soldiers tear down the granite obelisk commemorating the War of Independence. His tearful old father later told the pastor and anyone else who would listen that the lad had had no choice. He had been ordered to do it by Commissar Zhukov. So the pastor had been left wondering: what else had Zhukov told him to do?

"Actually, I was thinking that we should call the whole thing off," the pastor said.

"I hope your conscience is not bothering you," Mr. Männik said half jokingly.

"No, that's not it," the pastor said seriously. "I don't consider this a moral issue. It's our belongings we're removing, and besides, even if it's a little Jesuitical to think so, the Reds only said they were confiscating the farm, without mentioning the things in it."

"I certainly agree it's not stealing when you take back your own things, or rob the robbers," the clearly amused farmer said. "So what's the problem?"

"The problem is Jukku," the pastor said, and explained his reservations. "You've known him longer than I have. Do you think we can trust him?

"I think we can, but there's a lot riding on this, so if you have any doubts, we'll have to deal with them." He stopped talking to scratch the back of his head. "I'll tell you what. I'll figure out some pretext and bring him to the tavern for a couple of drinks. That way I can get him out of the way and keep an eye on Randar at the same time. Meanwhile you and the boys can go to the farm and load up the wagon and bring it back here and hide it in the barn. Then we'll set out for Suure-Jaani at midnight as planned. We'll take some of the old logging roads I know, so we won't run across any patrols."

When the twins returned to say that Randar was off to the tavern. Mr. Männik set off immediately to collect Jukku. "You'll have less than two hours to load the wagon, so you better get on with it as soon as you see us passing."

It didn't take long before Kingsepp and the twins were driving to the church farm. On the way the pastor was calm enough to chat casually with the twins, but the minute they reached the farmyard, his heart starting beating rapidly. Surely some random passerby would see them, he thought. But as they started lifting grain sacks and filling boxes with potatoes, cabbages, carrots and turnips, his fears disappeared and he began to experience a rush of excitement, what one might even call a pleasurable thrill. Later, on the road to Suure-Jaani, he began to feel apprehensive again, but as they neared the farm without mishap some hours later, he was almost ecstatic at pulling off their coup. Evely and Auntie Minna, whom they had not had time to alert, were startled to hear the wagon roll into the Metsa Talu farmyard, but were quickly reassured by the sight of the pastor and his three companions. They made short work of unloading everything into the barn, and after a cup of tea and some beef stew that the women hastily heated up, the four men set off on the return trip. It would be a race against dawn to get back, they knew.

As it turned out, they had one more day, which they used to transfer some livestock, before an order arrived instructing the pastor to be at the farm the next morning for an official inventory. By that time, the pastor and the Männiks had spirited away an array of tools, a cow and a pig, three hens and a rooster, as well as a third of the contents of the granary and the root cellar. They hoped that what they had left behind was sufficient to not overly strain credibility. The two functionaries who arrived at the appointed hour, accompanied by a uniformed soldier, were polite enough in a distant bureaucratic way, but it was clear from the start that they suspected something was not quite right. However, they didn't press the pastor for explanations, nor were they able to quiz the tenant farmer. Jukku had not been specifically required to be present, so Mr. Männik had sent him to Tallinn for the day on a trumped up errand. "I'm still not saying that he's not trustworthy, but he's a few grams short of a kilo, if you know what I mean. It would be better if he wasn't here," he told the pastor.

The functionaries nevertheless got their licks in just before leaving. They had seen the pastor ride up to the farm on Tasuja, and had insisted that the sleek-looking mare would have to be seized. The pastor tried his best to convince them that he needed the horse to do his job; moreover, he said, it had been a gift from his father, so could he please keep it? Although they agreed that he would be allowed to keep one horse, they said it wouldn't be that one, but another, which turned out to be the oldest, sorriest nag on the farm, one that had been retired to pasture at age twenty.

"Well, I think we got away with it," the pastor told Mr. Männik later, when he dropped by after the functionaries had left. "I'm only sorry about the horse, but maybe even that was for the good. They seemed rather pleased that they had been able to deny me something, so maybe they won't bother to look any further into why there wasn't as much in the barn as they had expected."

Chapter Nine

Two weeks later, Evely, who didn't want to miss the annual *Oktooberfest*, came back to Vändra for the weekend, leaving the children under Auntie Minna's care at the Metsa Talu farm. Eager to see the sights, she wasted no time in taking hold of her husband's hand and steering him toward the fair grounds. Having grown up in larger towns, she had always loved the way the village took on the appearance of a bustling market town for one week every fall. Hundreds of visitors from almost every farm and community within the parish would crowd the streets, coming to do the bulk of their annual shopping, to refurbish wardrobes and stock up on food supplies. The harvests were in, so it was also a time for rest and recreation. And because the spring lambs, calves and piglets were old enough to bring to the fall market, farmers usually had money to spend in the tents and booths that sprang up near the river.

This year, however, there was a very different atmosphere, Evely thought, attributing the lack of merriment to the strains caused by the Soviet occupation. The crowds were significantly smaller and many of the people seemed to be walking aimlessly, casting only cursory glances at the wares they passed. Few carried parcels or shopping bags. When friends met, they often just nodded a greeting, rarely stopping to chat or suggest going for a drink. Many wore the pinched, anxious faces more commonly seen at funerals than at a fair.

Nowhere was that change in ambience more evident than in the fields near the river where one would normally expect to find crowds of farmers milling around the livestock pens or wistfully eyeing the displays of new farm machinery. This year, it seemed as though many of the farmers had boycotted the fair, for there were far fewer animals, and the number of booths offering agricultural goods was at an all-time low.

It was the same story on the far side of the livestock pens where the bandstand and the games of chance and other entertainments were usually found. Most of the best rides were missing, among them the popular steam-powered musical carousel. "Too bad," Evely thought, staring at the booths piled with Communist Party pamphlets that had replaced the old attractions under a large banner proclaiming the virtues of Soviet Socialism and the brotherhood of the proletariat. In previous years, Evely had been tempted to go for a ride on the carousel, but Karl had always been reluctant, even when she had teased him about not wanting to make a spectacle of himself in public. She had liked to think that when the children were old enough, they would take a turn together on the colorfully-painted wooden horses. Now she wondered whether that would ever happen.

Closer to the river, on both sides of two long avenues were the booths that did most of the business of the fair and where Evely planned to spend most of her time. These stalls were mostly set up by farm women who offered a variety of homemade foods: preserves of all kinds, cheeses, sausages, baked goods, as well as embroidered linen, lace and knitted mittens, scarves and hats. Some of the men, too, had put to good use the housebound days of the previous winter and had items for sale that they had painstakingly crafted from bits of leather, wood or metal. But it was evident that there were many more sellers than buyers. Some of the artifacts were quite intricate and showed considerable artistic flair, Evely thought, but for her the biggest attraction was the booth of Maria Mõlder, whose delicate watercolors of Vändra landmarks she had admired for years. Maybe this was the year she would finally buy one for Karl's birthday.

As conspicuously missing as the carousel were the booths that usually offered a better cut of clothes and manufactured goods than were generally available in the village. Gone, too, were the booths that had featured fancy foodstuffs that buyers used to stock for the approaching holidays. Two years ago, Evely remembered, she had stumbled upon a kiosk that sold fresh oranges and bananas, exotic fruits she had never tasted. She could still remember the wonderful juiciness of the two oranges she had bought for Karl and herself, using up a considerable portion of the spending money she had put aside for the day.

As Evely and the pastor finished their quick tour of the fair grounds, Evely remarked to her husband: "Things are cheap, but I don't see very many people buying anything."

"People don't have much money this year," her husband answered. "The Russian policies have hit the farmers very hard, especially those who had big farms. They used to be the people with the money and now they have nothing. And the small farmers are suffering because of the ridiculous quotas and prices imposed on them."

The pastor stopped to say hello to Valdo Lillakas, one of the farmers on the church council, who was heading for the livestock pens. "We were just remarking how much poorer the fair is this year."

"You don't have to look very far for the reason," Mr. Lillakas said, pointing behind him at the beer tent past a row of stalls jammed with drab unsold goods from the Soviet Union. Like everyone there, the pastor had been all too aware of the grating voices of carousing Russians rising from the tent, and he didn't bother to turn his head.

"It's disgusting," Mr. Lillakas said. "Those damn Reds ... getting drunk and crowing while most of us can't afford even a glass of beer. Someone should tell them to shut their damn yaps."

Evely, who hated unpleasantness, excused herself. This was her cue, she thought, to slip off without Karl to check out Maria's watercolors. "I'm going to have another look at the handicraft tables, Karl. And then I think I'll go home to cook supper. But take your time. You don't have to rush."

After she left, the pastor and Mr. Lillakas were joined by Toomas Rebane, another farmer, who was also making his way to the agricultural pens, where the farmers liked to congregate to compare notes about crops and harvests and to appraise the animals. The pastor, who was curious to see how the new policies had affected livestock sales, decided to accompany them.

The air beside the pens was blue with pipe and cigarette smoke. "Not much here this year," one of the smokers said by way of greeting. "Not that it matters, since no one is buying."

53

"The whole market is like that ... the worst I've ever seen," a heavily bearded old-timer standing beside him volunteered. Both men spit on the ground to emphasize their disapproval.

"Oh, oh," Mr. Lillakas said suddenly to Mr. Rebane, pointing towards the beer tent. Seven grim-faced young Estonian men were purposefully striding in that direction. "Is that your son over there with his friends? I don't think they're looking for beer. Maybe we should go over there, too."

The pastor was aghast. "No, definitely not. That would be a serious mistake. The last thing we want is a fight," he said. "Let me go over there by myself. Maybe I can talk some sense into them."

As the pastor entered the tent, he saw that the Estonian youths had ranged themselves opposite a group of young Russian soldiers and were staring balefully at them in silence, as though daring the Russians to make a move. The Russians pretended to ignore them, but it was easy to see that they, too, were considering the odds and their options.

Some of the soldiers slumped on the benches had obviously been there for hours. "Well, if it isn't the Pastor," one of them called out slurring his words. "Come and have a drink. I'm buying." The man fumbled in his pockets and turned them inside out before mumbling with a sly glance at Kingsepp: "All gone. Too bad, Pastor. I guess you'll have to buy the drinks."

Several of the Estonian youths burst out laughing. "Look at the big shot. Thinks he's a big man, but doesn't even have an arse in his trousers."

Some of the Russians started to stand up, with fists clenched, as did the Estonians.

"Quiet, everyone," the pastor shouted in his most stentorian voice. "Sit down and listen. This is not the way to do things."

Just then, Karl Kivisik, wearing a militia uniform, entered the tent. Everyone could see that he had his sidearm strapped to his belt. "What's going on here?" he barked. "Pastor, why is everyone standing?"

The pastor forced a laugh. "We were about to settle an argument. You see, these lads both thought they were better singers than the others. So I suggested they each sing a song and we'd take a vote." He looked meaningfully at Kivisik, whose mouth turned up in a little smile.

"What a good idea," Kivisik said, letting his hand slide over his pistol. "In the interest of harmonious relations between all Soviet Socialist peoples, I'll buy a round for the winning side."

The pastor had to hand it to him. No doubt about it, Kivisik was quick on the uptake. "So who'll go first?" he asked.

Kivisik held up his hand. "Why don't the Vändra boys go first."

"How about it boys?" the pastor said. "What about singing '*Mu Isamaa on Minu Arm*?" He turned towards Kivisik, who didn't appear to be familiar with the song. "That's a local song, based on a poem by Lydia Koidula, who was born here in Vändra," he explained. Kivisik hesitated for a moment before slowly nodding.

The youths didn't need any further encouragement. The intensely patriotic song, a kind of unofficial anthem, obviously stirred their souls and they gave it a deeply moving rendition.

When it came to the Russians' turn, they couldn't agree on a song until Kivisik abruptly told them to sing "*The Internationale*." Most of them, it turned out, didn't know the words, or only parts of verses, as they stumbled their way to a ragged ending.

"Well, Pastor, who do you think is the winner?" Kivisik asked.

Kingsepp pretended to think for a minute, then turned his back on Kivisik to wink at the Estonian youths. "The local boys were more musical, but the Russians were better at projecting their values. So I have to give it to the Russians."

The obviously delighted Russian soldiers began to cheer and clap their hands. One or two of the Estonians looked bitterly at the pastor, but were nudged by their more perspicacious friends to also start clapping.

Kivisik held up his hand. "I think the pastor may have made a mistake. I would call it a draw, and since I promised drinks for the winners, that means everybody gets a drink."

"And that means you, too, Pastor," he said, adding more quietly so that only Kingsepp could hear, "Very cleverly done. Just don't try it again."

Chapter Ten

As the autumn of 1940 made way for the winter of 1941, the pastor thought it safe to move his family, together with Auntie Minna, back to the manse, leaving Evely's younger brother Mati to look after Metsa Talu farm. To his great joy and to some extent his consternation, Evely immediately confided to him that she was pregnant. It wasn't the most propitious time to bring another child into the world, but what time ever was, he thought. God would provide, but he was glad that Auntie Minna was now at the parsonage with them. Not only was she easy to get along with, but she had turned out to be far more energetic than he had believed possible for a woman of 62. She had helped look after a big manor house for thirty years, she said, so the upkeep of the rectory was a piece of cake. Best of all, by minding the two toddlers, who doted on her, she took much of the pressure off Evely.

The winter, like the previous one, was unusually severe, with many heavy snowfalls and prolonged sub-zero weather that kept everyone housebound for days on end. Even the occupying soldiers curtailed their patrols. Inside the manse, the Kingsepps spent most evenings in the large parlor where they kept wood fires going in both a stove and a large hearth. After the children had been put to bed, Karl and Evely often sat beside the fire reading, occasionally quoting for the other's benefit a line or two that had caught their fancy. Some evenings, when they didn't feel like reading or chatting, they told each other stories. Tädi, to their surprise, soon emerged as the most entertaining storyteller among them. Although she was normally quite reserved with other adults, Tädi had a rich store of humorous tales about her days in service with the eccentric Count von Mentzenkampf of Taevavärav Manor. The old man had been a bit of a holy terror with odd views about nearly everything. Although he was a martinet who never tired of showing his tenants and staff who was boss, he was also an easy mark for

57

practical jokes and rarely caught on when he was the butt.

Evely, who probably enjoyed these stories the most, never missed an opportunity to twist her aunt's arm, especially as her pregnancy progressed. On one of the darker and stormier winter nights, after dinner had been eaten and the children put to bed, the three adults gathered in the parlor around a blazing fire. Evely, who who was feeling a little under the weather, thought one of Tädi's tales would make her feel better. Her aunt was only too glad to oblige. Laying aside her knitting, she smiled at Evely and began: "This is one of my favorites. It's about the time when the old Count's eyesight was failing, but he still insisted he was the best hunter in his family."

"The more shots he missed, the more he wanted to prove himself," she said. "But things only got worse. His shots went all over the map, several times just barely missing the beaters, who became afraid to go out with him. The servants didn't know what to do because the old Count was too vain to wear glasses and insisted that the reason he kept missing his shots was that his gun was faulty. Changing guns with other members of the shooting party didn't help; they were all faulty, he barked. As his frustration mounted, he started getting more and more angry and threatened to dismiss his gamekeepers for incompetence.

"One day, when the Count had been more difficult than usual, a younger son of one of his friends, who had been dragooned into serving as a beater for the day, quickly sized up the situation. Borrowing a gun from one of the gamekeepers, he then suggested that the old Count change his 'faulty' gun with him. 'Let's go stand by that thicket over there,' he said, picking out a spot away from all the others. 'That's where we'll get the best shot.' He moved very close behind the Count, gently steering him towards the bushes he had pointed out. Sure enough, the beaters soon were able to drive a stag close to where they were standing. As the Count raised his rifle to his shoulder, the young man did the same, biding his time so that their shots went off simultaneously. 'Good shot, sir,' he shouted as the stag fell.

"'I knew the guns were the problem!' the Count shouted with glee. After that he always insisted that the young man accompany him on all his hunts. He also kept the old rifle, giving his expensive custom-made hunting rifle to the young man in exchange. And, you know what,"Tädi said, "he never failed to hit his prey again – until, that is, the young man got married and moved away."

They all chuckled. "What a smart lad," Evely said. "I can just picture the expression on the Count's face. It's too bad the Mentzenkampfs' manor house burned down and they all moved to Germany. We're probably missing a lot of good stories."

"Well, I for one am not sorry those days are gone," Karl said. "We Estonians were always too deferential to the German manor lords. Have you ever been in the Dome Church on Toompea Hill in Tallinn? I was ordained there, you know, but I guess it didn't register on me at first. Now I think it's a disgrace."

The two women looked quizzically at each other.

"No, not the church, of course, but the way the German barons had decorated it," the pastor, who had caught their glances, said with a smile. "The walls are practically covered with their coats of arms and pennants, but what's worse is the little cabin, if I can call it that, that they built for the governor in the chancel, almost beside the altar. You know, it's actually higher than the pulpit, which is pretty high to begin with, so that the governor was able to look down on the preacher. Shows you what their priorities were, eh? It's no wonder though, when you consider that the church in the old days supported the old feudal order. I think that was one of the things that convinced me not to join the Bishop's staff; I couldn't stand looking at those awful baronial crests every time we were in the church."

The ensuing silence caused the pastor to look around to where Evely and Tädi were both staring at the floor. "Sorry," he said. "I didn't mean to spoil the mood. Let's see if I can make it up to you by telling another story. Since you both think the barons are funny, I have one that's somewhat similar to Tädi's story ... but different, of course."

"You know that my father was a gamekeeper for the Count von Manteuffel in Jõgeva," the pastor began. "Manteuffel was probably a nicer man than your Count, Tädi, but he was also getting old and his eyesight was failing. Like your Count, he was a keen hunter, with a passion for hunting game birds, especially those that roosted in his oak forest. After several unsuccessful hunts, my father began to feel sorry for the old man and figured out a way to help him maintain his pride.

"The next time they went shooting, he got my older brother Aleks to go ahead and climb up a tree with a bird Isa had already shot. When the Count and Isa got close, Aleks was supposed to make a bird call, which he was able to do pretty well, making sure he was protected behind the tree trunk. To keep him extra safe, Isa would advise the Count to shoot somewhat to the side of Aleks' position.

"Isa was sure the plan was foolproof and it seemed to go off without a hitch. The Count fired and Alex dropped the bird. The ecstatic Count saw the bird flutter down and rushed over to claim his trophy. 'What the devil,' the Count muttered as he picked up the bird. 'This is most strange. I've never killed a bird before that came already wrapped.' You see, Aleks had forgot to remove the string he had used to tie the bird to his belt when he climbed the tree. So my father had to own up that it was all his doing. The Count, as I say, was quite a good sport, so he got a laugh out of it. But he never went hunting again."

"Well, I think that's a wonderful story," Tädi said, laughing. "But now it's time for me to go to bed." As usual, she liked to leave earlier than the pastor and Evely to give them a little time to themselves.

"Good night," Evely said. "Don't forget, Tädi, we're going to Maria's for afternoon tea tomorrow."

Social life was one of the few things that got an impetus from winter. The worse the weather, the more people liked to gather in groups around a warm hearth in each other's homes. Evely especially enjoyed the weekly afternoon get-togethers organized by the young mothers of the parish, where they would sip tea, and knit or embroider while chatting and keeping an eye on the children. At other times when heavier snowfalls kept people housebound, they kept busy preparing the traditional foods special to the upcoming holidays or making little gifts for each other.

Because many family members came home for the holidays, church services were always crowded, especially on Christmas Eve, when it was necessary to hold two services to accommodate everyone. Despite the extra demands on his time, the pastor was sustained by his vivid memories of the candlelit Christmas Eve choral services he had loved so much as a child: the reading of the Christmas gospels, the joyful singing of carols, the smiling faces and happy shouts of "Merry Christmas" followed by the sleigh ride home under a starry sky. And of course, the festive dinner and the distribution of presents, even if they were mostly clothing and a few sweets. For a child in a poor farm family, it was the highlight of every year, and he remembered how hard it had been to wait another twelve months for that magical holiday to return. Now, as an adult, he still looked forward to the joys of the holiday season and hoped that his Christmas Eve services stirred his parishioners, especially the children, in the same way.

That's why Kingsepp was very upset when he received a curt notice in early December that candles would no longer be permitted on the Christmas trees that traditionally flanked the altar at the Christmas Eve services. They were a fire hazard, the order from the commissar blandly stated. The pastor's initial plea for a reversal of the order was dismissed out of hand, but by persistently calling at the commissar's office, he finally got to see Kivisik, who grudgingly permitted the candles to be lit, provided two men with buckets of water stood beside the trees during the service.

The petty harassments continued through the holidays, picking up momentum with demands for more and more paperwork. Minutes of all meetings now had to be forwarded to the commissar, together with detailed financial reports and records of all his pastoral visits, everything in duplicate, of course. Miss Soosaar complained she could hardly keep up with the typing. To the pastor, who couldn't believe that Zhukov read any of those reports, it looked more and more like the Reds had chosen to kill the Church with a thousand little cuts, rather than in one fell swoop.

In early January, like everyone else, he was required to join the work parties sent into the forests for lumbering. His assignment was to trim the branches from the felled trees, a task he came to rather enjoy for the brisk exercise it provided. Most of the farmers, however, were not happy at being conscripted. The extensive Vändra forests had been a prime source of construction materials since time immemorial, and winter lumbering and milling had provided many parishioners with a considerable part of their annual income. That winter, because of the extra forced labor details organized by the Reds, as well as the regulated prices, the farmers were able to earn only a fraction of their usual take. Adding insult to injury, it was understood that most of the prime lumber earmarked for the Reds was going into the construction of an extensive network of Russian military bases along Estonia's Baltic coast.

Towards the end of January, when classes resumed at the secondary school, the village was shocked by the most disturbing incident yet. One of the new Soviet-approved teachers assigned his class of 16-year-olds an essay in which they were to describe how the Soviet system had improved the lives of Estonians. All but one of the children dutifully extolled the merits of Stalinist communism. That one boy had taken the subject to heart and honestly wrote that he considered life under the Republic to have been better.

The teacher decided to show the essay to Comrade Zhukov, who had the boy, Toivo Maasik, arrested. As soon as he heard of the situation, the pastor attempted to see the commissar to plead for the boy's release, but was refused a meeting. Again, it was Kivisik who eventually did see him, but only to say that he should forget about the matter since it had already been dealt with.

As usual with politically-motivated arrests, no one had seen the boy since his arrest. It was assumed that he had been sent to a labor camp in Siberia. The pastor decided that despite his resolve to steer clear of politics in church, he would make an announcement about the arrest and lead the congregation in prayers for Toivo – no matter what the commissar might think. As it happened, even the Red spies in the congregation refused to report the pastor's action.

By springtime, rumors were rife about events in the rest of Europe. The possession of short wave radios had long been forbidden, so no one knew with certainty what was happening in the outside world. But when Soviet news bulletins started leading off with German atrocities and downplaying the strength of the German army, villagers couldn't help but speculate about when and how they would be affected; after all, Estonia had often been the doormat when other countries had invaded Russia.

It didn't surprise anyone when the permanent garrison in the village was significantly strengthened and the number of army patrols increased. Villagers attributed the increased traffic on the roads to people hoping to get out of the way before any invasion took place. They also noticed that the patrols stopping travellers for identity checks seemed to be as much on the lookout for army deserters as for enemy agents. Most alarming, however, was the rumor brought by some travellers that a new round of civilian arrests was being planned in order to eliminate the threat of a fifth column when the war started.

Amidst the increasing unease, a happy distraction for the pastor's family was the birth and christening of baby Martin in mid-May. Pastor Kuusk, Kingsepp's old mentor in Pärnu, even managed to make the trip to officiate at the ceremony, which was followed by a reception at the manse. Tädi, with help from Evely, had scrubbed and baked for the occasion, and Mr. Männik contributed a barrel of homemade beer to go with the two bottles of vodka the pastor had convinced the village wineshop owner to sell him from his dwindling stock. One of Mr. Männik's sons brought along his accordion, and after the dinner, the pastor and Evely initiated a round of dancing with a waltz. "This proves you are the right pastor for us," Mr. Männik said. "There wouldn't have been any dancing in your predecessor's manse, I can assure you." For a few hours at least, the pastor and his friends were able to put aside their worries about the future, which several of them said, though not very convincingly, could only be better than the present.

Two days later, Kingsepp borrowed a gig from Mr. Männik and drove his family to Viljandi, where they would stay for a week in order to show the new baby to Evely's parents, who had been unable to attend the Christening due to her mother's illness. Then, until they were certain which way the wind was blowing, Evely and the children would again settle in for an extended stay at Metsa Talu farm. The pastor himself came back to attend to parish business.

Chapter Eleven

On Sundays, because he was still careful to avoid being anywhere on his own for any length of time, Kingsepp usually tried to arrive at the church when it was already filling up with worshippers. That Sunday, however, he was late, having slept over at a distant farm where he had gone for a Christening. By forcing his old nag to increase the pace as much as he dared, he managed to arrive on time. As he rushed to don his vestments in the sacristy, his eye was caught by a small piece of folded paper pinned to his cassock. When he hurriedly glanced at the unsigned penciled message, he felt his heart begin to beat faster: "Be careful. They're planning to get you this morning."

There was no time to waste, but Pastor Kingsepp felt rooted to the floor, even as he heard the final notes of the familiar Bach prelude, the one Johannes Vares, the organist, played in rotation every third Sunday.

The pastor peered anxiously around the slightly ajar door of the sacristy. It didn't take him long to spot the stranger. Like many farmers in the congregation, he wore a rumpled "Sunday best" black suit, but unlike them, he had an unsmiling, hard-looking face. It didn't seem as though he was there to hear God's word, the pastor thought.

"O God, our help in ages past..."

Cued by the organ, the congregation had started singing, some of them looking towards the altar, only a few steps away from where Kingsepp was standing, still undecided about what to do. It was a good thing they couldn't see him, he thought. *"Get hold of yourself,"* he muttered. It was probably nothing to worry about, just another in the ongoing attempts to harass and intimidate him.

"Our hope for years to come..."

On the other hand...? Maybe he should pretend to be ill, just stay there until someone came to check on him. But could he really do that? Was he a coward?

65

No... he would call their bluff; and if it wasn't a bluff... well, there was only one way to find out. In any case, he was sure he would not be in any danger until he turned his back to face the altar during the recitation of the Creed.

Slowly, very deliberately, not wanting to stumble, he stepped out. A quick glance at the back of the church confirmed that the stranger still sat quietly by himself, still looking fixedly towards where he now stood. His somewhat stained suit jacket was rather ominously buttoned despite the summer heat, he noted in a sudden surge of panic.

"Be Thou our guard while troubles last,
  And our eternal home."

The words of the hymn gave him pause. He didn't *want* to go to his eternal home today! He was too young, with a lot of life ahead of him and he wanted to see it unfold. What would his young sons and his daughter become? He and his wife had talked about having even more children... and eventually grandchildren. Even Jesus had asked his Heavenly Father to spare him.

But, of course, Jesus hadn't been spared. So why should he be? He squared his shoulders and tried to look serene as he opened his missal to begin the liturgy. He sensed that his voice was catching slightly, but not so that anyone would notice, he hoped. Soon, he realized, he would have to turn towards the altar. What if he didn't? Would anyone notice, or care, if he stayed facing the front? Was that the answer?

But God would know. Could he live with the knowledge that he was a coward?

As he worked through the last paragraphs of the familiar text, he kept one eye on the back of the church. The light was poor back there, but despite the gloomy shadows, he felt the stranger's stare as an almost physical force. For sure, the stranger was no churchgoer; he didn't seem to know the liturgy, or chose to remain silent when a response was required. Then again, that might not mean anything. Most of his congregation only mouthed or mumbled the responses, like those fidgeting youths also sitting at the back.

They were from distant farms near the edge of his parish and seldom attended services. He remembered all three of them, always hanging out together, as particularly disruptive students in his confirmation class, was it four or five years ago? Only there to impress the girls. He had heard they had since been in trouble for drinking and fighting. Well, maybe he could set a better example for them today, show them what kind of man a Christian could be...

Starting suddenly, he realized that he had been going through the liturgy on auto-pilot and that it was time to turn towards the altar.

He hesitated, took a deep breath and slowly pivoted. He fixed his eyes on the large painting that was the backdrop to the altar, a crucifixion scene of Christ surrounded by four women, including Mary, His mother, at the foot of the cross. He stared hard at the face of Christ in His agony, before lifting his gaze to the gothic-lettered banner above the picture: "Glory to God on High."

He squared his shoulders and hoped he was standing especially straight, as he began to recite the Creed. He tried to concentrate on the words, pronouncing each one carefully so that his voice would ring out strong and clear. But he hardly knew what he was saying, feeling only the coldness of the sweat running down the small of his back.

It came as a shock to suddenly hear the congregation singing out their amens. The liturgy was over; he could turn around again.

As his eyes landed on the empty place in the last pew near the center doors, his knees buckled slightly and he had to take an extra step to avoid stumbling. "Thank you Lord," he murmured as the organist struck up the hymn that would precede his sermon.

After the service, smiling, but still somewhat dazed, he stood at the door to shake hands with the outgoing congregation. He barely heard the voices praising his sermon.

"You outdid yourself today, pastor." "A powerful sermon." "It's too bad those Reds aren't here to listen...They might have learned something."

As the congregation filed past him, he noticed the three youths still lingering in the side aisle. When the last of the congregation had made their exit, they shambled forward, the biggest and roughest-looking one at their head. A sudden thought struck Kingsepp almost like a hammer blow. "Oh God, no, it couldn't be possible... not them...." He watched them approaching as though in slow motion.... He saw the hand come up slowly ...

"I hope you weren't worried, Pastor. We picked that Red out right away. We were ready for him," the first youth said, slowly pushing aside his jacket to reveal the pistol in his waistband.

Chapter Twelve

Although she missed Karl, Evely found that staying at Metsa Talu farm was pleasant enough. It was cozy here, she thought, and brighter than at the manse. And she was beginning to really enjoy Tädi's company. Her aunt was more like a big sister or a friend, not at all like her own mother, who never wanted to talk about any of the things that interested Evely the most. Here, she could sit in the kitchen for hours, sipping tea and chatting with her aunt about whatever came into their heads while the children played contentedly on the floor. She smiled at Jaak, nearly four, who looked up at her every few minutes while happily playing with his wooden blocks. Anna, twenty-two months, was kneeling nearby, making faces at Martin, her baby brother, who was lying on a blanket on the floor cooing with delight. Tädi, as she was wont to do periodically after her husband's death four years ago, was leafing through a photo album, pausing to sigh as she looked at pictures of her husband. It hadn't always been clear to her, but now that he was dead, she realized how much she had loved being married. Peering over her aunt's shoulder at the album, Evely could see Jüri, half hidden behind his large mustache, standing rather stiffly in a brand new suit beside the armchair where Tädi sat in her Sunday best muslin.

"Did you think he was handsome?" Evely asked. "Is that why you married him?"

"Oh, we didn't think about things like that," Tädi replied with a slight coloring of her cheeks. "I was getting on to sixty when we got married. I just liked him for being so gentle. We never argued, you know. And I think he liked my cooking. At least he said he was tired of the same old thing he had been making for himself all those years."

"And what about you? Why did you marry Karl?" Tädi asked, turning the tables. There was a moment's silence.

"Singing brought us together," Evely finally said with a laugh.

"Do you want to hear the story? It's rather long." Her aunt wasn't fazed. "Then why don't you put the children to bed," she said. "I'll make us a fresh pot of tea, and we can have some of the buns I baked this afternoon."

A half-hour later, with steaming cups in front of them, Evely, still smiling, began her tale. "You know, of course, how much we Estonians love singing, especially choral singing. I always used to sing in school concerts and I remember when we once went to the *Laulupidu* choir festival in Tallinn. That was amazing... 20,000 voices singing together. I hope you've been there, Tädi, because no one should miss that.... Well, we'll have to go once all this nonsense is over," she added after Tädi had ruefully shaken her head. "Anyway, after I finished high school I didn't sing for a few years, but I missed it. People kept telling me I had a good voice, so I finally joined a church choir in Viljandi where some of my friends were already members."

"As it happened, " she said, "the choir was invited to a choral festival in Pärnu city, where the local church organized billets for us. In return, our choirmaster had promised that we would sing at the Sunday service. Oh, you should have seen it," Evely told her aunt. "The church was very large and it was crowded, not only with the congregation, but with at least a hundred or so singers from other choirs.

"And there was this young pastor who was so funny. What really struck me was that he couldn't sing a note. But he didn't seem to know that. He just kind of bellowed out the hymns at the top of his voice. He was totally unselfconscious. I couldn't help myself; I had to put my hands in front of my face and laugh. It must have been quite obvious, though, because my friend Mari told me not to embarrass her."

"But all that changed moments later, " she said, "when the pastor climbed up to the pulpit to deliver the sermon. I saw a totally different man, the real man, I believe... It was astonishing. His eyes lit up. He was so eloquent, so interesting, so sure of himself, so handsome..."

"Would I be correct in assuming that you are referring to your Karl?" her aunt interrupted, smiling broadly.

"Of course, of course...How did you guess?" Evely said with a giggle. "I'd never seen such a change in someone. I was intrigued ... I thought I would like to meet him." Evely went on to explain that, even though she hadn't planned to, she went to the reception after the service. He was there, of course, busy talking to small clusters of choristers. While conversing with her friend Mari, Evely kept glancing secretly in his direction. He was of average height, but somehow, because of his confident bearing, he appeared taller. And he had lovely blue eyes.... After a few more discreet glances, she noticed that he seemed to be eyeing her, too. Then, to her surprise, he started to make his way in her direction.

"He looked so serious, I thought he was coming over to castigate me for laughing at him during the hymns. I didn't want to be embarrassed by him, so I thought I would slip away before he got too close. But he was too fast for me," she said with a laugh. "With a quick flanking movement, he blocked my escape and just stood there looking at me without saying a word. I was too flustered to do anything but look down at my feet. I just hoped he would go away."

"So you're Evely Lepik," he finally said. "I was told that you are the best singer in your choir. But I noticed that you are an even better music critic." Then he introduced himself. "My name is Karl Kingsepp. I'm the assistant pastor here."

"I don't know why I blurted out what I did. I even surprised myself. 'Everybody knows that.' And then I made it worse by saying: 'Well, I did think you could use a good singing teacher.'"

"I thought he'd be angry with me, but he wasn't. He just told me he'd look into that and maybe I could give him a recommendation. Then he said he would get me a cup of coffee and a piece of cake."

"So it was all your doing," her aunt said. "Good for you. I would never have had the nerve."

"Yes, that's how it began," Evely said, smiling. "Two weeks later, Karl drove to Viljandi to talk to my father, who was delighted to see that I had a suitor. However, I wasn't too happy when Isa told me that a pastor wouldn't be his first choice for a son-in-law. But we couldn't afford to be choosy, he told me."

"Your mother always said that Kalle was a bit silly," her aunt broke in. "I'm glad you didn't pay any attention to him."

"Why would I? Karl was much more interesting than any of the fellows I had ever known. And he wasn't stuffy. He had a great sense of humor and we always had fun together. We even went dancing."

"Anyway, we ended up married and Karl was "called" to Vändra, so there we are now..."

"I guess the first time I met him was after Jüri died," Tädi broke in, "Remember, I asked you to ask Karl to conduct Jüri's funeral. I thought Karl was a very nice man and that you were lucky to have him."

"He is a good man," Evely said, "but I don't think he quite knew what he was getting into. In less than a year, he got married and acquired not one, but two sets of parents-in-law. Then there was this farm, and he started a new job at one of the largest parishes in Pärnu province. It must have been quite overwhelming."

"And now with the Russians here, he has a lot more to worry about," her aunt added. "It certainly hasn't been easy for him."

"I don't really want to think about that," Evely said. " Why don't you tell me another Mentzenkampf story, Tädi. Please?" After spring had arrived, there had been less time for stories and Evely missed her aunt's animated recollections of the old Count's antics at Taevavärav Manor.

"I told you that he was rather vain, for no good reason anyone could see," Tädi began. "He liked to think he was another Casanova, a bit like your father, I think. Anyway, he was quite upset that in his sixties he was starting to go bald. I guess he thought he would lose his touch with the ladies, so he went to all kinds of doctors and tried all kinds of remedies, but with no success. Soon he was quite desperate and was very happy when his steward, who was a practical joker, told him he had heard of a faith healer, a very old and very wise woman who lived in a little village just beyond his estate."

"The steward knew exactly how to entice the old Count. He told him that this wise and holy woman had cured the Tsar himself of baldness. He even showed him a picture of the Tsar with a full head of hair with lots of nice curls.... I think it was actually a wig," she added with a laugh.

"Well," she continued, "the Count could hardly wait for his carriage to be brought around. When he came back, he called his steward and told him to go immediately to the chicken coop and fill a jar full of chicken droppings. The steward pretended not to understand, and the Count got quite testy. 'I need the droppings to rub on my head, you numbskull,' he said. 'Have you ever seen a bald chicken? The old woman assured me that it's the only surefire method for growing hair.'"

"Well, off went the steward and came back shortly with a jar full of the softest, greasiest, most foul-smelling chicken droppings that he had been collecting for weeks for just this purpose. The Count looked a little queasy and asked for a perfumed handkerchief he could hold to his nose."

"'Now rub it into my scalp,' the Count commanded, 'and put a gauze plaster over it so it won't fall off.... It has to stay there for a week in order to properly fertilize the scalp.'" Tädi could not contain herself any longer and had to stop for a few moments until her laughter subsided.

"Well, all the next week, you could smell the Count coming from 100 meters away. No one would sit near him. He had to eat all by himself. No one invited him anywhere. But he was so happy and kept telling the servants, who could not avoid him, how all the ladies would be chasing him next week."

"Of course," she said, "when the gauze was untied and the putrid mess cleaned off, there was no sign of any new hair. The Count was perplexed. He was sure he had missed some part of the instructions and wanted to go back to the wise old woman -- who had been in on the joke, of course – but old Rosenkranz, the German pastor, was used to these shenanigans, and managed to put him off."

After some more hearty laughter, both of them sat back to catch their breaths. In the momentary silence they suddenly heard hoofbeats turning into the farmyard. "Who could that be?" Evely asked, going to the window to shift the curtain to the side. "We're not expecting anyone.... Ah, it's Karla. I hope it isn't bad news."

Chapter Thirteen

"I don't think I have ever been more frightened in my life," Kingsepp told his wife at the dinner table while he absentmindedly stirred the hastily warmed-up fish soup Tädi had put before him. His experience in the church that morning had clearly unnerved him. All day long he had wanted only to hug his wife and children and had waited impatiently until dark to ride the 20 kilometers to Metsa Talu farm along the back roads that Mr. Männik had shown him. "I was sure that was going to be my last hour on this earth, and I could only think of you and the children. I didn't want to die. I remember when I was very young reading about all the martyrs who had died for their faith and thinking how heroic that would be. But it's very different when you're actually in that situation. I felt something like St. Augustine who wanted to be saved, but didn't want to give up his pleasurable but dissolute life – just yet! It's an unimaginable horror to have it all come to an end, without seeing the children grow up, to never see you again; it's ….." His words trailed off as emotion overcame him.

"Do you think Zhukov put that man up to it?" Evely asked after a brief silence. "I can't bear the thought he wants to kill you. You can't go back there, you know. You'll have to stay here, or hide in the woods."

"No, I don't think it was Zhukov," he replied. "He would have had me arrested by his soldiers. But who knows how anyone will act these days? I had never seen that man before, but that doesn't mean anything. The NKVD have all kinds of agents who move around doing their dirty work."

"Lucky for me that the lads were there. It was strange though… because I've never seen them in church since their confirmation four years ago. They must be involved with the *Kaitseliit* militia or the partisans. What else could it be?" He shook his head. "I still can't believe he was thinking of shooting me in the church, in front of everybody. I was so sure I'd always be safe inside the church."

They sat in silence for a few moments, mulling it all over.

"Things are definitely getting worse," Evely finally said. "Isa got a letter the other day from Hilda. She went to Tartu, you know, to be closer to Mark. She said my brother's unit has been ordered to Russia for some kind of training. Apparently all the Estonians are going. She thinks it's part of a plan to completely absorb the Estonian Army into the Red Army. Anyway, they have no choice, and wives and families can't go with them. Hilda's really worried."

Karl frowned. "She's right to be worried. It can only mean one thing. The Russians are getting ready for war and they're going to use our soldiers at the front. This is not a good time to be an Estonian soldier."

"Hilda also says," Evely interjected, "that the Germans will come through here to get at Russia. We're all going to be caught in the middle."

"Between the anvil and the hammer," the pastor added. "We've been hearing a lot of terrible things about the Nazis, so I doubt we'll be any better off under them, if they win. But that's all hypothetical. As long as the Reds are here, we have to worry about them."

"I agree," his wife said. "So I say we should all stay here. Obviously it's no longer safe for you in the village."

"Yes," Karl said. "I was planning to do that, at least until we can figure out what that thing today was all about. Mr. Männik said he thinks that it might have been just one man, some kind of vigilante who has a bee in his hair about religion. We all know there are a few of those people around who are taking advantage of the Reds being here to work off their grudges. Anyway, he's going to try to check with the Forest brothers and maybe even with Kivisik. He'll let me know if he thinks it's safe."

"There's something else to consider, too," he told Evely after a pause. "If the commissar is really after me, I'm not all that certain that they wouldn't find this place. And, if they traced me here, you'd be vulnerable too. That's why I think I might be better off in the parish, where I have friends who can help me."

Evely nodded. "Even so, you should at least wait until you hear from Mr. Männik. That will give us some time to be together and you'll be able to see the children."

As she spoke, she glanced at her aunt, dozing quietly in a corner of the kitchen, then lowered both her voice and her gaze. "It's nice to see you again, Karla," she said as a winsome smile flitted across her face.

Karl felt a stirring in his heart. They had seldom been apart since their marriage. Once, less than a year after their wedding, he had gone on a month-long motor trip to Hungary for a gathering of Lutheran pastors. He could still remember how lonely he had felt despite the many interesting sights and events he had experienced, how much he had missed her. As she looked shyly up at him, he nodded and smiled back.

Chapter Fourteen

It didn't take long for Mr. Männik to get back to him. One of the twins arrived mid-morning on his third day at the farm to say that no one knew anything about the stranger in the church, not even Kivisik. So most likely, he was some kind of lone vigilante or fanatic who had strayed into the parish and left quickly when he realized that there would be no easy pickings for him there. The pastor decided to spend another night with his family and go back early the following day.

The next morning in Vändra, when the pastor was unsaddling his horse in the small shed where he had kept the old nag ever since the confiscation of the church farm, he heard Jukku calling from a distance: "Is that you, Pastor?"

The shed was ramshackle and out of the way, a fair distance from the manse. That was the reason he had chosen it as a safe place to bury a few carefully wrapped altar pieces, especially the chalice and candlesticks dating from the 17th century when the parish had been founded. They were of no great monetary value and worthless to the Reds, but he had been worried about ideologically-motivated vandalism and thought it prudent to hide the irreplaceable heritage items. One night, when he thought no one would be about, he had buried them under the dirt floor, over which he had then strewn some straw and a few old boards. That morning, he had impulsively decided to check whether the cache was intact. Jukku's unexpected arrival flustered him and he hurried to cover his tracks.

"I just wanted to make sure it was you, Pastor," Jukku said as he reached the doorway. "I've seen a man skulking around here the past few days, and I thought maybe someone had come to steal the last of the animals."

"Yes, Jukku, it is me," the pastor answered, adding somewhat testily, "Who would want to steal an animal like this?" as he pointed at the wheezing old nag he had just ridden.

"Well, that's all right, then," Jukku said, turning to leave. But then he stopped. "They found a body this morning. You should be careful, Pastor, especially on the roads at night."

Later that morning, while working on a sermon in his office, he received a puzzling phone call from Karl Kivisik. "Major Zhukov wants to see you, but don't worry," he told the pastor. "There are no plans to arrest you...yet."

Was that a joke? Kingsepp was worried, but he knew he had no choice but to go. At the village offices, the same clerk who had done the inventory of the church farm asked him to wait "a few minutes." He became more worried when the few minutes stretched into a half-hour. What was Zhukov up to? Every time he raised his head to look at the wall clock, he saw Stalin staring back at him. Beside the "man of steel," Lenin also fixed him with a piercing gaze. It was hard to get used to those thugs usurping the places of Konstantin Päts, the last President of a free Estonia, General Johan Laidoner, the Estonian army's chief of staff, and Jaan Tõnisson, a four-term elected prime minister – the holy trinity of heroes of the Estonian Republic, whose portraits had "disappeared" for the past year-and-a-half, like the men themselves. God save them, wherever they may be, Karl thought. He was still sitting there a half-hour later, hunched over with his elbows propped on his knees, his hands supporting his chin, staring morosely at his shoes, when he heard his name called.

When the pastor entered the spartanly furnished inner office, Yüri Zhukov had his back turned and was barking something into the phone. But within a minute, he had swiveled his chair around, slammed the phone down, leaned back, and with a scowl motioned the pastor to sit. Without his interpreter, he spoke in halting Estonian. As usual, he didn't stand on ceremony.

"You know there has been another killing, yes?.... One more Russian murdered. One in Viljandi; one here. That is two in two weeks, plus poor Vassily. What do you people think? You kill one every week and get rid of us in ... um... (he stroked his chin) ... one hundred years?"

Zhukov seemed to be momentarily amused by his own wit, but then slammed his fist on the table. "This must stop. I am telling you

80

no more. There will be consequences, and you, my friend, will be the first to suffer. We don't want any teachers of false values making trouble here."

Kingsepp was shaken by Zhukov's vehemence and kept silent. He much preferred dealing with Karl Kivisik, whom he had despised at first for being a traitor to his people. But since then he had learned that if you caught Kivisik alone and in the right mood and at the right time, he could be almost friendly. He had even been helpful occasionally, as with the Christmas candles in the church. Mr. Männik had also told him that Kivisik had once helped some farmers who had fallen short in their production quotas. Apparently some rubles had discreetly changed hands that time, something the pastor found puzzling. As an ethnic Estonian who had cast his lot with the Reds, Kivisik himself was sure to be under considerable scrutiny by his bosses. Was he so greedy he'd risk being sent to Siberia for the small sums involved? Anyway, why wasn't he here now?

Staring intently at the pastor's face, Zhukov suddenly asked: "You were on Viljandi Road last night? This side of Suure-Jaani, yes?"

Pastor Kingsepp met the commissar's searching gaze with a steady look of his own, but said nothing. There was a quiet knock on the door, and a head peeked in.

"Ah, Karl, you are back? Okay, I have to go to Tallinn now. You talk to your friend, this other Karl, yes?" Zhukov said before rising and leaving the room. As soon as he had left, Karl Kivisik entered, chuckling. "Got you worried, didn't he? I don't think you are guilty, but Zhukov is angry. He is still thinking about poor Vassily who fell off your motorcycle ... and now that "visitor" at your church the other day? But pastors don't do such things, do they?"

Kingsepp had to think for a moment, before he caught Kivisik's drift. "Why did you mention what happened at the church?" he finally asked. "Was that man the victim? Do any of you really think I murdered him?"

Kivisik was evasive. "Anything is possible. But there is a problem; that's why we have to question you. You see, we don't know the victim. He has Russian identity papers, but no one here has ever seen him before. No real Russian would go to church unless for a reason. So you or some of your people probably know him. Anyway, I want you to take a look at him. He's out back, in the shed."

Kingsepp got up reluctantly. It wasn't the dead body that bothered him; he had been at hundreds of deathbeds. His concern was of a different nature. If they couldn't find the murderer, and they probably wouldn't if the partisans had been responsible, they wouldn't care whom they arrested – as long as they got someone. If not him, then whom? Obviously, he couldn't tell Kivisik about the three young men who had been in the church.

There was no sheet over the naked body and there wasn't much ice around it either. But plenty of flies were hovering, particularly around the face and the stomach area where the man's intestines and most of his blood seemed to have spilled out.

Kivisik nonchalantly brushed the flies from the victim's face. "Well, is it him or not?"

Kingsepp knew right away that it was the same man despite the slack jaw and vacant eyes, but he was shocked by the degree of violence that had gone into the mutilation of the body. He pretended to study the face carefully, before speaking. "He was a long way from where I was, and sitting in the shadows, so I can't be absolutely sure, but I think it is him."

"Of course it is," Kivisik said angrily. "I only wanted you to confirm that, and for you to see what kind of barbarians your people are. You call yourselves Christians? Well, we'll show you what that means. When we find the murderer, and we will, Zhukov will nail him to a cross."

"I can't believe you think someone from the church would do a thing like that ... to any man," the pastor said earnestly after a moment's silence. "Some of our people may not like your regime, but this is not our way. We've been taught to love our neighbors and to turn the other cheek."

Kivisik ignored the pastor's comment. "You know what really interests me?" he said more calmly, pointing to the victim's stomach. "How he was killed. This is not an ordinary murder. It looks more like the work of a madman or someone trying to send a message. Why else go to the trouble of mutilating the body like that?"

The pastor shrugged.

"I don't usually agree with you," Kivisik continued, "but I don't think it looks like the work of your partisans. They like to hit and run; they don't hang around, carving up their victims. So who else could it be? And what message is he trying to send? We want you to help us with that because Comrade Zhukov wants to wrap this up quickly before Moscow gets wind of it. One way or another, he will do just that."

Chapter Fifteen

As he rode in a light drizzle towards the Allisma farm the next morning, Pastor Kingsepp mulled over his conversation with Kivisik. He had chosen a round-about route, one that added a half-hour to his trip, but he had taken to heart what Kivisik had said, especially what he had said about Zhukov's desire to close the file one way or another. It was all very confusing. If Zhukov and his gang didn't know the victim and hadn't sent him after me, then who was he? Who had warned me and why? Had the murdered man really been after me? Who had killed him and why? Why had Juhan Allisma and his friends, who never go to church, been there that day?

Jogging along on the old nag was a bone-jarring form of torture, he decided. He wished he still had Tasuja, the speedy young mare the Reds had taken from him. Now that was a horse! On her, a long ride like this would be a pleasurable outing. About a kilometer from the farm he came around a bend to find Juhan's grandfather mending a fence beside the road. *"Tere, Pastori Härra,"* the elderly man said, doffing his cap. "Not such a fine day for a ride, is it? Or did you lose your way?"

"Tere, Osvald," Kingsepp answered, reining in the nag. "These roads are pretty tricky, but, no, I'm not lost. I'm actually looking for your grandson. Is he home?"

"That depends on who's looking for him and for what reason. But since it's you, Pastor, I can say that he is at home. You might try looking for him in my son's new barn. If you don't know where that is, it's another kilometer past the farm, a bit into the woods, so you'll have to keep a sharp eye out." Having finished his little speech, the old man turned back to his work. "Well, Pastor, it looks like there is more rain on the way, so if you'll excuse me, I have to finish banging this post in." As he spoke he picked up his hammer and gave the tin-topped post three sharp, resonant whacks.

With a nod and a thank you, the pastor rode on for another fifteen minutes, past the Allisma's farmyard to the edge of the encircling woods. Once he got closer, he could just barely make out a building behind a screening thicket. If you didn't know of its existence, you could easily pass it by. It was rather small to be a conventional barn, and it had discreet windows under the eaves on each side that commanded a good view of the road in both directions. A good spot, but for what? he thought. As he dismounted, he saw a strongly-built young man emerging from behind the barn. Obviously he had expected a visitor and had been keeping watch.

"Ah, Juhan, there you are," the pastor said in response to the young man's greeting. "I came to thank you for the other day. You probably saved my life. I'm very grateful, but you left so quickly I didn't get to thank you properly. And then I thought, I know, I'll ride out and give each of you a Bible. Everybody should have a Bible of their own. It can be a great consolation when things aren't going well."

There was an awkward moment of silence, but then Juhan smiled. "We were happy to help out, Pastor. I'm sorry you had to come all this way for that, but thank you for the Bibles. I'll pass them on." He seemed to think that ended the conversation, but Kingsepp wasn't finished.

"Actually, Juhan, I do have something else to say. You know that I usually try to stay away from politics. So, tell me if I'm barking up the wrong tree, but it seems to me that you and your friends might be in serious trouble. No, no, let me finish.

"Commissar Zhukov called me in yesterday for a very strange conversation. You may already know this; a Russian was found dead on the Viljandi road yesterday morning. Turns out he's the same man who was in church on Sunday. What's strange is that neither Kivisik nor Zhukov has any idea who he is. He has Russian identity papers but no one has ever seen him before."

The pastor could see from the agitation on Juhan's face that he was about to say something.

"Juhan, please. I do want to hear what you have to say, but I haven't quite finished. I just need another minute, and then you can speak all you want."

"What was even more strange," the pastor continued, "is the way this man was killed. Not only was his throat slit, but someone went to a lot of trouble to slice off some of his fingers and to disembowel him, probably with a bayonet or some such weapon. I'd like to believe that it wasn't you and your friends who did this."

Juhan couldn't hold back any longer. "It wasn't us, Pastor. What do you think we are?" Juhan, who had become agitated during the pastor's description of the body, could hardly control himself. "I know we don't go to services often, but that doesn't mean we're savages. How can you even think that?"

"Calm down, Juhan. I'm sorry if you took it that way. Of course, I don't believe you are savages. I just wanted reassurance, because you're the only people I know who actually had any idea what that man was up to ...and you had a gun and presumably you were ready to use it. So, I wanted to hear it from you."

"Yes, I did have a gun and if he had lifted a finger against you, I would have used it. But don't you understand what you yourself just said? I had a *gun*, but you said he was murdered with a *bayonet*. It couldn't have been us, don't you see? We didn't follow him. None of us ever saw him again after he left the church."

"Juhan, listen to me. This could be a matter of life and death. If we don't want Zhukov to turn on our people, we have to convince him that we had nothing to do with this murder. I need your help. You have to tell me everything you know about this man – when you learned what he was up to and who told you, and anything else you know."

"I have no problem with any of that," Juhan answered without hesitation. "It's very simple. No one told us. We don't know who put it there, but Tõnis found a note pinned on the driver's seat of his parents' wagon when he went to harness the horse for their trip to the church. He does that every Sunday, so it was someone who obviously knows his routine. Anyway, he was worried because his father had told him you had been threatened before. So Tõnis told me, and I suggested he should also get Andres and the three of us would go to the church.

"When we got there, we knew everyone except the stranger in the back, so we sat nearby to keep an eye on him. When you were reading the epistle, he started to reach inside his jacket. That's when I coughed to catch his eye and opened my jacket to show him the gun. He left right after that, so I guess he was the guy all right. Anyway, that's all I can tell you. The rest you know yourself."

Pastor Kingsepp, who had kept his eyes fixed on Juhan the whole time, was convinced the young man was telling the truth. "What exactly did the note say? Can I see it?"

"No, I burned it. We didn't want to have anything connecting us to that man."

The pastor frowned. "What about what was written?"

"Like I told you, it said only that someone was going to be in church that morning to 'get' Pastor Kingsepp. It was written in Estonian."

Kingsepp sighed. His own note had said pretty much the same thing, so there was no new information there. "Hmm...One last thing. Did you or the others tell anyone else about the note, either before or after?"

The young man shook his head. "We all agreed beforehand not to tell anyone about what we were doing, just in case. So I don't think anyone else knows anything about this, except you... and I guess whoever wrote the note ... and the killer."

Two days later, the pastor still knew nothing more. After talking to Juhan, he had visited several other farmhouses in the northern reaches of the parish, an area of thick woods and treacherous swamps that stretched for tens of kilometers. Rebels and outlaws had found refuge there in the days of the German Brothers of the Sword, and that's where the *metsavennad* tended to hide out. More than a few members of the banned Volunteer Militia (*Kaitseliit*) had taken their weapons and vanished into the thick forest after the Reds had purged their leaders and ordered all Estonians to turn in their firearms. These forest brothers had built camouflaged bunkers, usually on small islands of solid ground in the middle of the many bogs that dotted the area. During the day, if all was clear, they would go back to their family farms to help with the work, returning at night to their hideouts in the woods. If anyone asked for them, their families said they had gone to visit relatives in far away places.

Kingsepp knew that the local farmers would know what the partisans were up to, and hoped that some of them might even tell him. But when he had tried to discreetly raise the issue, no one knew anything. Not even the usually helpful Valdo Lillakas, at whose farm he had slept. "It's best not to know too much these days," Valdo had said, echoing what all the other farmers had told him.

Kingsepp knew better than to push any harder. People were afraid, and he was sympathetic. Besides, he had started to wonder what he would do with any information he might get. He couldn't very well betray any confidence that would lead the Reds to the partisans or to Juhan and his friends, if indeed they had been responsible for the murder. So what exactly was he trying to find out and why? It was only for his own sake, he decided. After all, there had been a mysterious attempt on his life. Surely he had a right to know what that was all about.

Chapter Sixteen

At the Lillakas' farm next morning, after a breakfast of oatmeal porridge and boiled eggs, Valdo and his son Erik had gone off to work in the fields while Kingsepp took over the kitchen table to put in a little work on his sermon for the upcoming Sunday. It was the only table in the house, so when Mrs. Lillakas came in from the yard he thought she was reclaiming the table to make lunch. He started to gather up his papers, but she shook her head and handed him a folded note. "Erik went to the village for nails and Jukku gave him this message for you. Must be important, I guess, all sealed up like that."

She was obviously curious, but the pastor just thanked her, making no move to read the note. After an awkward pause, she murmured, "I have to feed the hens," and left. A few minutes later, Kingsepp emerged from the farmhouse and seeing Mrs. Lillakas nearby, told her he was sorry he would have to skip her kind invitation for lunch, but he had to leave immediately for the village.

Two hours later he was at Jukku's small cottage on what used to be the church farm. A military car was parked to one side. Even from a distance he could hear the angry voice of Karl Kivisik loudly berating Jukku. "You must know where he is, you miserable oaf. I want to talk to him now. Go find him."

"No need for that. I'm here," the pastor said on entering the two-room clapboard cottage. "I just got the message. And by the way, it's quite true that Jukku did not know where I was. And you should know why."

"Yes, yes, yes," Kivisik said a little less loudly. "Now get out," he shouted at Jukku. "I don't want to see you around here before I leave."

Kingsepp sighed. He could see that this was not going to go well. "I'm sorry, but I have no new information. I would have contacted you if I did. I did check, but nobody knows anything about the murdered man."

"Spare me the excuses. As it happens, that's all water under the bridge and I'm no longer interested. There are more serious things to worry about now."

"Do you mean you found out who he was and who killed him?"

"Oh, stop it. I told you I am no longer interested. No, we have not solved the case. We know he was carrying false papers, so he could have been anyone, an Estonian or some other Balt, or even a German spy. But Moscow doesn't know anything about this case, so it doesn't matter.

"Zhukov doesn't care anymore, so neither do I. A lot has changed since last Sunday, and I need to talk to you about something else. But first, let's have a drink. I brought some real brandy, from Georgia. Try to find some glasses; I don't like drinking from the bottle, unless I have to."

Kingsepp's inclination was to decline the drink, but he didn't want to anger the man. Also, he had heard that Kivisik liked to conduct his business over a drink, especially when there was something important at stake.

He knew Jukku always used a tin mug himself, but after a bit of rummaging he found two drinking glasses on a shelf behind a Bible, the only book in the cottage. The glasses, as well as the Bible, had belonged to Jukku's father; and from the thick gummy dust on them he guessed neither had been used since the father had died a dozen years ago. Finding a relatively clean shirt in a small heap of clothes beside Jukku's bed, the pastor did his best to wipe the grime off the glasses.

Kivisik, who had already taken the bottle from his briefcase, almost beamed when the glasses were produced. "That's why I like you, Karl. Despite all the religious claptrap you spout, you're practical, at least sometimes. So, here we are: Two Karls. Two KKs. Friends, I hope," he said, pouring out two sizeable drinks. *"Prosit!"*

Kivisik raised his glass towards the pastor before downing it in one gulp. While Kingsepp took a small sip, Kivisik poured himself another half-glassful.

"So why did you want to see me so urgently if it isn't about that murder?" Kingsepp asked.

Kivisik silently contemplated his glass for a few seconds, smiled and took another big swallow. "You know people like to think everything will always stay the same. But time marches on. Situations change. People change. Nothing stays the same forever. Look at us here. Right now I wear a uniform and sit behind a big desk and you have to do what I say. You have no choice. But will it always be like that? Things can change. Next week, you might sit behind the desk and I'd have to do what you say, eh? That's how life is. We never know...."

This was beginning to sound very odd, the pastor thought. Where was Kivisik going with these thoughts? "I don't follow what you're saying," Kingsepp said.

"It's very simple," Kivisik said. "The Germans are coming. And it won't be long before they are here. They're already in Latvia and will start bombing us soon."

"Don't look so surprised. You're not naïve. You must know that Uncle Joe and Uncle Adolf are not pals despite their friendship pact. Stalin has never trusted Hitler. He knows that Hitler has always wanted to turn the Baltic into a German lake, so it was only a matter of time until his army would march."

This was important news, the pastor thought, but why would Kivisik tell him this? What did he want from him?

Kivisik poured yet another shot for himself, no longer pretending they were sharing drinks. "I can see the wheels turning in your head," he said. "Yes, I do want a favor from you." The pastor grimaced.

"Don't be like that," Kivisik said. "Look, I've seen the messages from Moscow. They don't believe they can hold back the Germans, so we're all going to be evacuated. But before that, Stalin wants us to make Hitler's advance as hard as possible. That means a scorched earth policy here. We're being ordered to destabilize the Baltics by dismantling bridges, railways, factories, anything that might be useful. Whatever can be packed up and sent to Russia will be; the rest will be destroyed. Special "destruction battalions" are being formed to do whatever is necessary to achieve this, and there will be more purges and deportations.

"Zhukov is sorry he didn't pack more of you off to Siberia. He doesn't think it will look good for him if Moscow thinks he has been too lenient. More than half of the "enemies of the people" on the list he was given are still here. So he's probably going to try to fix that before he's evacuated.

The second shoe was dropping, the pastor realized. "Why are you warning me?"

"Don't interrupt me," Kivisik said. "I'm coming to that, but first I have to fill you in on the big picture. There's a lot at stake in this for both of us."

"You see, Zhukov thinks we will be fine once we get back to Russia, but I don't believe that. Even if he ends up in an office somewhere, the rest of us will be used as cannon fodder at the front. Russia is overmatched; unless Uncle Joe throws everything he has against his old pal Adolf, and I mean *everything*, he's going to be skinned. As far as I'm concerned, being sent to the front will be a death sentence, so what am I to do?

"I've thought about it quite a lot, you know. I've never been like the others. I'm really not a bad guy. I had to follow orders but my heart was never in it. When I could, I tried to help your people; you know that. So maybe now you can help me. I can make myself disappear until Zhukov and the others have left, but then what? I can't hide forever. I need someone to vouch for me – someone with authority, someone whom the Germans would believe."

What a hypocrite, thought Kingsepp, who was beginning to see which way the wind was blowing. How could he possibly believe I would help him? Even if he wasn't the worst of the lot, twelve people have already disappeared from this village, and are probably breaking rocks right now in Siberia. He was part of that process. He's just a scumbag, desperately trying to save his own skin.

"Tell me one thing, Karl," the pastor said. "You say you are not like the others. You are Estonian, yet you work for the Russians. How is that possible?"

"I'm surprised at you, Karl," Kivisik answered. "You of all people should understand. Like you, I was born poor. So how does a poor Estonian boy get ahead?" Kivisik grinned and looked straight at the pastor. "The Party is my church."

"Look, Karl," Kivisik continued, "I know this is a shock to you and I know that you probably don't trust me, but I'm serious. I saved your hide at least twice this past year. You were among those earmarked for arrest when we arrived, you know, and Zhukov was ready to get rid of you. Who do you think persuaded him to hold off? I told him a professor at Tartu had earmarked you as a good candidate for heading our religious directorate. Pretty clever, eh? But I nearly got into a lot of trouble when you refused to play ball. There was nothing I could do to save the others, but at least I managed to save you."

Kingsepp's head was reeling. Was he still alive only because of this man? A man he had been accustomed to seeing as his enemy and a traitor to his people? Was he supposed to feel gratitude, when what he really felt was revulsion? He was in a daze and hardly heard Kivisik's next words.

"We don't have much time. If Zhukov wants to clean the slate here before the destruction battalions arrive, he has to move now. I've copied out a list of his targets – twenty-two persons and, yes, you're right at the top. If you agree to help me, I'll give you the list and you can warn everyone to take to the woods for a couple of weeks until the Nazis arrive."

Kingsepp knew he was being manipulated and he didn't like it. Usually, when he had serious decisions to make, he would take time to gather all the pertinent information and then pray for the wisdom to make the right decision. How could he make up his mind responsibly in these circumstances? There were so many things to consider. Since Kivisik surely would not want anyone else to know about his apostasy, a refusal to help him would surely lead to his own death. Would he be aiding and abetting a criminal in order to save his own life? Twenty-one other souls had to be considered as well. Did he have the right to jeopardize them in order to indulge his moral scruples? Was there even a clear-cut solution?

Kivisik looked quizzically at the silent pastor as though trying to see what lay behind his dazed eyes. "Look, *Härra Pastor*, when I say we don't have much time, I mean that. I need your answer now. I know you can't speak for your *Kaitseliit* and *metsavennad* friends, but you can talk to them. They might want to kill me no matter what you say, but I'm willing to take that chance because I know they respect you in this village and because I know you will do your best to keep your word. In return, I'll make sure Zhukov doesn't find any of you before he leaves."

Kingsepp remained silent. He was still weighing the pros and cons, and praying for guidance. It bothered him greatly that Kivisik seemed to know him as well as he knew himself. Even if he couldn't believe everything Kivisik said, it did seem that he could save the lives of at least 21 of his parishioners, as well as himself. Wouldn't he owe Kivisik something for that?

Taking a deep breath, he began to speak: "How much can I trust you? I've been asking myself that, but that's not the right question. What I have to ask is 'What would Jesus do in this situation?' I did that and I think I now know. Jesus came to replace the old 'eye for an eye and tooth for a tooth' ways with a new message of loving your neighbor and doing unto others as you would have them do unto you. So even if I find it hard to love you, I'm going to follow His example. Give me the list now and I will do my best to provide the support you have asked for. Will you agree to that?

"Yes, I will," a visibly relieved Kivisik said quietly.

Chapter Seventeen

Although the conversation with Kivisik had left Pastor Kingsepp mentally worn out, he knew he shouldn't waste any time before warning the others on the list. As soon as Kivisik had driven off, the pastor hurried to Mr. Männik's farm, hoping to find him or one of his sons at home. They seemed to know everyone and everything of any consequence in the parish and would know exactly what to do. Fortunately, Mr. Männik was at home and instantly understood the urgency of the situation. "We have to get everyone on the list into a safe place. Luckily, the woods are deep enough to hide them all. It won't be a problem, if we move quickly.

"So that swine Kivisik wants to save his skin," Männik added after a moment. "Who was it who said there is no honor among thieves? Every man for himself, eh? I have to say he's an enterprising fellow though. I don't think I could have come up with a plan like that. Anyway, Pastor, no one can blame you for shaking hands with that devil. You may be taking a risk, but I suspect God is watching over you."

"I do believe that," the pastor said. "You know, I was surprised you weren't on the list, Mr. Männik; everyone knows there aren't any stauncher Christians in this parish. You should be extra careful in case it was an oversight."

"Ah, why would they bother with an old fellow like me? I haven't held any official position for years, so they probably don't even know I exist. But we can't afford to dawdle, so let's get started. I'll send one of my boys to Suure-Jaani to let your wife know you're safe. I'll take care of all the details, so you should go straight to Allisma's farm. Juhan will meet you there and take you to a safe place. God keep you, Pastor." He clasped the pastor's hand and held it for a moment before letting go so the pastor could mount up.

Kingsepp had always been surprised by how quickly messages and news spread from farm to farm. He had stopped at the rectory for less than a half-hour to pack a small bag and pick up a few books, but sure enough, by the time he got to Allisma's farm, Juhan was already waiting for him near the barn. After a brief greeting, he was all business; still respectful, but clearly expecting the pastor to accept his authority as a group leader of the forest brothers, something that the pastor had only lately realized. "We know you're public enemy number one right now," Juhan said, "so we have to be very careful. You're going to follow me, but first I want you to unsaddle and leave your horse here. Someone will bring it to your pasture so it won't lead anyone here. Then we're going to go into a part of the woods you've never seen; it's a bit tricky to get there, but that's why it's the safest place we know."

When Kingsepp had finished tying up his horse, Juhan nodded at him and without a word started walking. Kingsepp followed. There was no trail through the thickly overgrown evergreen forest. As he picked his way confidently through the underbrush, Juhan kept a steady pace that left the pastor slightly winded. He'd have to give up smoking, he thought. After a while, he noticed the ground was getting springy and then somewhat sodden. Juhan slowed down and chose his footing more carefully now, indicating to the pastor where he should step. Every now and then they had to cross a pond, stepping on rocks artfully placed just below the water line. Occasionally Juhan would make a bird call, answered in the distance by similar sounds. They had passed several likely spots for a bunker – mound-like islands of solid ground covered by thickets – but still they kept going.

They had almost passed another of those islets, when they heard the familiar birdcall close by, which Juhan answered. Almost as if by magic, he saw three bearded men emerge from a thicket to greet Juhan.

"So this is our new guest," one of them said. "I'm Andres. Welcome to our humble abode," a remark that sparked great amusement in the others. "Yes, you're right. I should really say welcome to our luxury hotel. All the comforts of the Baltic Barons at your fingertips – if you can find them under the water."

"That joke's getting stale, Andres," Juhan said. "Let me introduce you to the Pastor."

Andres, it turned out, was an officer in the *Kaitseliit* of a nearby village. A strongly built man of about thirty with a cowlick and a constant smile, he was an explosives specialist whom the Russians had long been after for blowing up one of their armored trains. He had been taken in by the Vändra men when it got too hot for him at home.

Endel stepped forward next. He was from southern Estonia, a *Soome Poiss* (Estonian volunteer who had fought in the Finnish Winter War against the Russians) who had made the risky decision to return to Estonia to take up arms for his own country. He had almost been captured in Tallinn during a routine identity check, but he had managed to outrun and hide from the Soviet patrol. He was on his way south to see his parents and was slowly being moved along the "underground railway" by various forest brother groups.

The third man had hung back, but now stepped forward. He was someone the pastor knew very well, Toomas Sillaots, a scoutmaster and a history teacher at the Vändra secondary school. His name had been high up on the commissar's list, the pastor remembered. Toomas was not a churchgoer and the pastor had had a few run-ins with him soon after his arrival in Vändra. Kingsepp had complained to the scoutmaster about taking his boys to the Kaitseliit rifle range on Sunday mornings. The steady staccato of rifle fire was disrupting the church service, he said, but Toomas had refused to stop the practice, saying that Sunday was the only time the boys could use the range. He was a patriot, he had told the pastor, and the nation needed its sons to learn survival skills. Ever since, there had been a coolness between them. Now, however, he stuck out his hand and said, "Well, Pastor, I guess we're on the same team now." Not really, the pastor thought. *We may both be on the run from the same enemy, but I'd like to see some change of heart on your part before we can be on the same team.* But he took the proffered hand and said mildly, "Hello, Toomas."

They went inside the bunker, which was lined by rough planks and had space for six bunks and not much else. "Two more people will be joining you as soon as Tõnis can get them here," Juhan said.

99

"We're your contacts with the outside, so we're not staying. I think for the time being you will find you have everything you need. But we'll be dropping by from time to time with more supplies. One more thing: Toomas knows this area and helped to build this bunker, so he will be your leader. It's very important that you listen to him carefully, because we expect a destruction battalion to make a sweep through this area soon. They probably won't come quite so deep into the bush, because they don't like to stray too far from their vehicles, but you never know." After taking Toomas outside for a brief private conversation, Juhan wished them well and disappeared into the forest.

As the four men sat quietly on their rough bunks in the dim light let in by the half-open hatch of the bunker, Toomas explained "the drill" they would be expected to follow. Basically they would rise with first light and retire when it got dark. They didn't have to stay inside all the time; it was too dark and damp, and too small a space for that. They could go outside to read or for other quiet activities, but should be ready to get under cover at a moment's notice. "If any of you are smokers," he said, "sorry, but that is strictly forbidden everywhere, and there can be no lighting of fires, for obvious reasons. However, we do have a small Primus stove for making tea." Everyone would have to look after his own possessions and weapons, but they would share all the chores, including lookout duty. On most days, they would spend a few hours reconnoitering, following the roads from the edge of the woods. Men from the four other bunkers in the Vändra area would be doing the same thing in their territories, and they would all gather if any action were to be taken against a Russian convoy or patrol. "Of course, Pastor, we don't expect you to participate in any fighting," Toomas added.

The pastor looked at him in surprise. "You forget that I did my military service like everyone else, and used to hunt as a boy with my father who was a gamekeeper," he responded somewhat tartly. "But it is true that since becoming a pastor I have been a pacifist. Nevertheless, if I am reconnoitering with you, I would make an exception if it were necessary to defend myself or others."

"Bravo, Pastor," chimed in Endel. "We're always on the defensive in this war. By the way, was that bird call for us?"

Toomas got up to climb out of the bunker, repeating the bird call as he went. He soon popped his head inside to say the other two men had arrived with Tõnis. They turned out to be Kalev Teras, another former teacher at the secondary school, and Osvald Puusepp, the non-medical director of the local hospital, both of whom were on Kivisik's list. Kalev, the pastor knew, had been close to Toivo, the student who had been arrested for his "anti-Soviet" essay. "I guess that's why they put you on the list," he said after greeting the newcomers.

"I don't think so," Kalev answered with a nervous laugh. "I think it's because I'm named Kalev. After all, isn't that what our national epic *Kalevipoeg* promises – that Kalev will return one day to free Estonia. They probably think I'm coming to chase them out." He must have noticed the flicker of disapproval on the pastor's face, for he immediately added, "I don't mean to be flippant, Pastor. It's become a kind of defensive mechanism for me recently. I was quite close to Toivo and I still can't bear to think about what they've done to him. He's not strong like Juhan or some of the other lads, but he couldn't bear to do or say anything dishonest. He would never compromise his principles, and look where that got him!"

Kalev swallowed hard in an effort to control his emotions. "I can't see him lasting long in the *Gulag*. When I think about that, all I want to do is kill the Red bastards. But at the same time I don't want to end up being like them."

"I understand," Kingsepp said. "I too pray for Toivo every day. Unfortunately, that's all we can do."

The next morning, Pastor Kingsepp awoke with the sun, but found that the others had been up for at least half-an-hour. He had had a hard time getting to sleep on the narrow planks that served as a bunk, and had to scramble to get up in time for a hot cup of tea from Endel, who was on "kitchen" duty that morning and was already doling out slices of bread and hunks of cheese.

After the men had eaten, they set off to reconnoiter, with Toomas in the lead. When they returned several hours later, Toomas and the two militia men were hardly winded, but the pastor and the two slightly older newcomers were breathing heavily. At least it had been an uneventful day, for which the pastor was thankful.

The next four days were equally quiet, but then they received an unexpected visit from Juhan who, along with more provisions and rifles for the pastor and the other two newcomers, brought them the news they had dreaded to hear. Kivisik's warning to the pastor had been borne out. Only days after they had taken to the woods, NKVD agents and destruction battalion units had set out to round up the so-called subversives in Vändra. Angry that most of the prime suspects had flown, they had arrested a dozen villagers, almost at random – probably just to fill their quota, Juhan said.

Similar purges had been carried out all over Estonia, he had heard, as well as in Latvia and Lithuania. Over the space of two nights, Juhan said, thousands of these alleged "enemies of the people," sometimes together with their wives and children, had been packed off to Siberia in cattle cars. In the past two years in Estonia alone, he said, the underground Kaitseliit leaders in Tallinn had estimated that more than 20,000 people had been purged by the Reds.

What was most disturbing, Juhan said, was that the special battalions had started their destructive work. In fact, he said, one of their informants had told them that a squad of "destruction battalion" soldiers was scheduled to arrive in Vändra the next morning. The *metsavennad* from another bunker were going to ambush them at the village of Ojasilla, but they needed help. Only experienced men were wanted, Juhan said, so the three newcomers would have to stay behind in the bunker. Toomas, Andres and Endel would have to set off immediately in order to get into position before dawn.

Almost twenty hours later the three men returned, looking tired and bedraggled. They had seen some action all right, they said, but not what they had expected. Because they had not had any sleep and were dead on their feet, they said they needed to rest a bit before telling their story.

While the three men napped, the pastor and Kalev resumed the chess game the men's arrival had interrupted. They were well matched; although Kalev was a pawn up, the pastor had a better board position and the outcome was not yet predictable. Osvald, who didn't play but wanted to learn, was content to watch them. About two hours later, just minutes after Kalev had conceded the match, Endel started to stir and soon all three of the sleepers were up, drinking tea and eating hunks of bread and cheese, while the others hovered around.

"Well, the *kuradi* convoy never showed up at the bridge," Andres finally said after gulping down the last of his tea. "I had my charges all set and we would have nailed them all right, but they must have been warned."

Toomas picked up the tale from there, saying they had waited until noon, when a messenger arrived on a bicycle to tell them the Reds were now coming by another road near Selja village. If they hurried, they could set up a new ambush. Because most of the *metsavennad* from the other bunker had come on bicycles, he said, they were able to speed off to Selja right away.

"Those of us who had to go on foot didn't get there in time," Toomas continued, so only about five men were in place when the convoy arrived. Nevertheless, they opened fire on the troop transport and killed three of the Reds before they were driven off by machinegun fire. Our friends had to run for it into the woods. Luckily only one of them was hit, a flesh wound in his thigh, so they all got away. When the rest of us arrived about 20 minutes later, the Reds were already gone.

"We caught up with the other fellows and we all went together to Vihtra village, where we heard that the same group of Reds had just passed through. They must have been feeling really mean because they killed an old farmer and set his farm on fire after catching him listening to a shortwave radio. One of the villagers told us that a forest brother had also been killed by them a bit further down the road, but we couldn't get any confirmation. Jaan is trying to check that out now."

"Anyway, we learned that the Reds were seen setting up an overnight camp on the banks of the Pärnu River at Kavasoo. They probably think they're far enough away to be safe, but we think they're vulnerable from the other side of the river. So we're going to attack them there before they attack us."

"This time," Toomas said, "we're going to need every man we have. Of course, if any of you don't want to take part in this, you don't have to go," he added, turning to look at the pastor. "So try to get some rest now because we're moving out before sunrise."

Toomas' dig at him had been uncalled for, the pastor thought as he lay on his bunk with his eyes closed. He didn't think he would be able to sleep at all, but a tug on his arm woke him up just after midnight. No one seemed to be about except Endel, who was looking down at him. "I thought you might want to come with me," he heard Endel say. He explained that they had found the body of the forest brother killed by the Reds and were going to bury him right away before they left for the attack. "Everyone else has gone, and Toomas said there was no need to wake you, but I don't agree with that. I'm a stranger here, but from what I understand there are good reasons for you to be there. First, I want to offer you my condolences..."

Kingsepp was startled. "What do you mean?"

"I'm sorry; I'm doing this all wrong. Let me start again. The dead *metsavend* is Sulev Eidepere, who I understand is a member of your church."

"What?" The pastor was dumbfounded. "He's just a kid. Of course I want to go to his funeral. In fact, I should be burying him. Where is he now?"

"I think that's the problem, Pastor. There's a grove of oak trees, a *hiis*, not too far from here and Toomas insisted that we bring the body there. He said that because Sulev was a follower of the old Taara religion, the burial must be done according to Taara rites. He said that if you knew about this you might try to stop them."

"This is unbelievable," the pastor said. "His father used to be a member of the church council and Sulev was in my confirmation class just two years ago. How could he be a Taara follower?"

"I don't know, Pastor. I'm just telling you what Toomas told me," Endel replied softly.

"Well, I want to be there. Regardless of what Toomas says, I think Sulev would want me to say a prayer for him before he is buried. Can you take me or show me the way? Don't worry, I won't cause any trouble."

With Endel leading the way, they went deeper into the forest, carefully picking their way without a light. Despite what Toomas and the others might believe, Kingsepp was familiar with Taara religious practices. He didn't even think there was anything inherently wrong with them, just that they fell short of what Christianity offered.

After walking for about twenty minutes, they saw a flickering light through the thick underbrush ahead. As they got closer to the oak grove, he could smell the aromatic juniper and cedar twigs smoldering in a brazier placed at one end of a large flat rock. On it, too, he saw Sulev's body laid out, dressed in a medieval-style tunic, with an old-fashioned sword between his clasped hands. A dozen or so men stood with heads bowed in a circle around the rock, listening to Toomas, dressed in a long white robe and a skullcap of criss-crossed strips of leather, intoning a prayer.

They had approached quietly and no one seemed to be aware of their presence outside the circle of light. "I think I'll stay here for the time being," the pastor whispered to Endel, who also made no move to go forward.

The scene evoked a long-forgotten memory in the pastor's mind. He was fourteen and had gone home for the term break after a year of secondary school in Tartu. He had been full of himself, he later realized, and had filled his brother's ears with all the amazing things he had already experienced and what he still hoped to accomplish. His brother, who like their father seldom spoke much, had looked at him rather disappointedly before saying, "Don't get me wrong, Karla, I think it's great that you're so enthusiastic. It doesn't even bother me that you seem to be so interested in living in a big house and moving up in life; but it worries me that you might easily become one of 'them.' You know that we were a people with our own values and ways of seeing and doing things long before the crusader knights came and started imposing their ways on us 700 years ago. That's something that you should never forget." A few days later, Karl had accompanied his brother to a *hiis* near Jõgeva to witness a midnight Taara ceremony. He had no intention of changing his plans for the future, but had been surprised by how much the sibilant cadences of the Taara priest's prayers had moved him. Now, as he stood in the shadows of the forest, watching the raptly listening men, he again felt the power of atavistic emotions.

The blood of the ancients
runs through our veins;
The forms may change
But life's circle remains.

Make my inner flame burn bright
Sustaining light through the night;
Part of my people, I will always be
And my people are a part of me;
A single flame of many parts
All of us with but one heart.

We all come from the Goddess
And to her we will return;
Whether flesh, bone or horn;
All that dies will be reborn;
So it is with fruit and grain,
All that falls will rise again.
The blood of the ancients
Still runs through our veins
The forms may change
But life's circle remains.

"That's what our forefathers believed; that's our heritage," he heard Toomas say. "And so it shall be for Sulev. Do not feel sad for him. He will be born again and will rejoin our struggle to free our land. With the sword of Lembit we will drive out the enemy who are sullying our shining birches and mighty oaks. So walk with wisdom and renewed strength, not sadness, from this hallowed place. This morning, when we go forth to do battle, Sulev will be watching over us. Let us honor him as he expects us to."

Kingsepp waited until the men had shouldered Sulev's body and started a slow march to the already-dug grave he had passed on the way to the *hiis*. Silently, he fell in behind Toomas, before whispering his name. "I didn't interfere with your ceremony," he said. "Now, I would like to say a prayer for Sulev at the grave."

Toomas didn't show any surprise. "I saw you in the shadows," he said. "I expected you to try to stop our 'pagan rituals,' but you didn't. I thank you for that. And since he was your parishioner too, I see no reason why you shouldn't say a prayer. I don't think any of the men would be opposed. They're not all Taara believers, you know, but they take comfort in a Taara warrior's funeral rites, especially when they might be facing death themselves."

After the burial, as they returned somberly to the bunker, Toomas walked alongside the pastor. It was obvious that he wasn't looking for a conversation so much as a chance to vent what was on his mind. He had a lot to say, as though the dam holding back his thoughts had finally broken and the words were rushing out in torrents.

"You know, I think I might have misjudged you, Pastor. Your church has been fighting our Taara beliefs for hundreds of years, so we have had no reason to trust any of you. Most of us can't afford to be openly Taara. I wouldn't be allowed to teach at the secondary school if I was. And I certainly wouldn't be allowed to be a scoutmaster corrupting the innocent Christian minds of our children. So I have to practice secretly and to pretend to be Christian. That's not very hard to do, by the way. Your people don't have to do much except attend service once in a while and get married and baptise their children. Anyway, for us, the real ceremonies are performed at the *hiis*. We don't think there is any harm in a little extra Lutheran water."

He wasn't far wrong, the pastor thought. He knew what many of his parishioners were like: Christians in name only, attending church only during the holidays. He had been trying to change those habits, but it wasn't easy.

"Anyway," Toomas continued, "isn't the point of all religions to guide us through life, to make us better people? Does it really matter what religion anyone is? Why do we have to belong to an imported religion, one that was imposed on us with a sword by German invaders? Only in the last while have people like you started to replace those foreigners. But why don't you and the others replace their foreign religion as well? Why can't we all get together to practise our own Estonian religion? People like you should be helping your own people reclaim their heritage."

"I have no intention of defending the past practices of my church," the pastor broke in. "It's quite true that the German pastors supported the feudal system, but the religion that we practise now has no similarity to what went on before. I don't have anything against Taara beliefs as far as they go, but they lack the deeper substance of Christianity. They are hollow at the core: just a romanticization of a mythical golden age that never existed. At least, that's how I see it. I have no faith in some vague spirit of the earth."

"I didn't really expect to convert you, Pastor," Toomas said. "You're a nice man, but you're full of foreign ideas; you've lost your Estonian identity. I hope it's not too late for you, however. Estonia is in crisis and needs men like you."

They were almost back at the bunker. "I have a lot more I want to tell you, but we'll have to continue this conversation later," Toomas said. "Right now I have to get ready to fight the communists. You don't have to come with us, but we could use your help in the rearguard. You'll only have to fight if we bite off more than we can chew. Then your job would be to cover our retreat. We're leaving in two hours, so what do you say?"

Kingsepp didn't hesitate. He knew from his year of military service that he didn't like fighting and would never want to be a soldier. As a pastor, he was also opposed to killing, but he believed that evil had to be resisted. What could be more evil than the Reds' "destruction battalions" that raped and killed and like locusts destroyed everything in their path? They had to be resisted. If it came to that, he knew he would be able to break the sixth commandment.

It was a three-hour march to Kavasoo, where the attack would take place. With the two others in the rearguard, the pastor took up a position about 100 meters behind the main attack group and followed at that distance until they were told to stop and hide themselves behind some natural cover about 150 meters from the river bank. The others crawled forward silently to the edge of the river and took up prone shooting positions behind stumps and whatever other cover they could find.

It was still dark and only flickering shadows from the dying embers of the Russian campfires indicated the presence of the enemy tents. Two sentries had been posted at the far end of the camp, on the land side, where they obviously felt they were most vulnerable, but they appeared to be dozing. For the next hour, an eerie silence prevailed, until at first light a few birds started calling, eliciting answers from others roosting in the surrounding trees. As the light became stronger the *metsavennad* looked at Toomas, expecting the signal to fire at any moment. When the guards stood up and a few shadowy figures began to emerge from the tents, Toomas blew his whistle. The volley of rifle fire was followed instantly by a loud whirring of wings as dozens of birds rose to escape the violent intrusion into their space. From his position in the rear, Kingsepp could see Russian soldiers struggling to get away from the tents to the shelter of the thickets behind them. Several – he couldn't see how many – fell before they reached the woods. Within minutes they had manned their machine guns and were firing back a more deadly fusillade than the metsavennad could manage with their bolt-action rifles.

He heard the prearranged signal to retreat blown by Toomas' whistle and waited for all the men to pass him before following. He had kept track of the men and knew they were not all accounted for. Looking back, he could see two bodies on their side of the river and started to go back for them. He had hardly taken three steps before he had to take cover from the heavy firing from across the water. "Don't be a fool," he heard his companions calling to him, "there's nothing you can do back there except get yourself killed." He looked back ruefully, made the sign of the cross, and rejoined his comrades at a run.

They kept going for at least a couple of kilometers before Toomas called a halt. "I think we killed at least five or six of them, so they're hurting, but sooner or later they are bound to come after us. I'm going to go across the river for a little "recon" and will be back in two hours. In the meantime, I want two of you, Endel and Ado, to sneak back on this side to see if you can reclaim our two casualties. If anything goes wrong, everyone should go back immediately to the bunkers."

Endel and Ado were back before the appointed hour, each carrying the body of a forest brother. There was no sign of Toomas, however, even after they had waited another hour. "I don't like the look of this," Endel said. "Toomas would not be late if he could help it. I'm going back to check it out."

Less than an hour later he was back, looking miserable. "It's like I feared," he said. "Toomas is dead. His body's hanging naked from a tree where they had their camp. It was hard to see clearly, but I don't think he died an easy death. We'll know better when we collect his body tonight. The *kuradi* Reds seem to have moved out, so I think that'll be safe enough. But we should get away from here now."

After they had moved off some distance, the *metsavennad* stopped to consider their next step. All the men, including those from the other bunkers, decided that Toomas and the other two victims, should be buried near where Sulev had been laid to rest. Meanwhile, they would try to gather more precise information about the location of the destruction battalion, and then hold another meeting to plan how to deal with the enemy soldiers who were threatening their homes.

Chapter Eighteen

Pastor Kingsepp conducted the funerals for the dead men, including Toomas, as no one offered to take up the mantle of Taara priest that Toomas had worn. "We're not really Taara believers," Andres told him, "but we all admired his patriotism, so we humored him." Neither the pastor nor anyone else had any idea who was Toomas's next-of-kin. He had never married and had lived with his widower father until the latter's death two years ago. Kalev, who had taught with him at the Vändra high school, said that once, when someone had asked him why he had never taken a wife, Toomas had answered that he was already married to the cause of Estonian freedom. "I don't think he cared much about anything else," Kalev said. "If it's all right with you, I'll go through his rucksack to see if he has a will or anything like that here." Within minutes, Kalev came out of the bunker, waving an envelope. "It's addressed to you, Pastor," he said. "I guess you're the stand-in for next-of-kin."

Toomas had softened his attitude towards him the last few days, the pastor knew, but this was a complete surprise. "If you don't mind," Kingsepp said after opening the envelope, "I'd like to read this by myself." He had noted in his quick perusal of the lengthy letter that instead of resting before going off to battle, Toomas had spent his last hours writing what seemed to be a confession. It was obviously written hastily, in a messy scrawl that was sometimes hard to decipher, with words crossed out or written in the margins in several places. Some of the passages were underlined, as if to ensure that the reader did not overlook their significance:

Dear Pastor, the letter began...

In a few hours we will be going into battle and only Taara knows how that will turn out. If you are reading this, it's because I didn't make it back. I thought about this for a long time and decided that I could not die without telling anyone what I learned from that Russian who was found dead on the Viljandi road. You might already know all about it, so this letter may be unnecessary, but I can't afford to take that chance, so bear with me.

You know who Lembit is, of course - the first real hero of our people, who almost succeeded in repelling the German Brothers of the Sword back in 1217. You've probably seen his monument in Suure-Jaani. He's depicted in a sitting position, dying, but still looking up to the heavens. In his right hand he is holding aloft his sword. He hasn't given up; he will fight to the end. Well, that's our inspiration, the example I have always held up to my boy scouts and to my comrades in the Kaitseliit. It may sound foolish to some, but I, and many others, believe that whenever Estonian hands hold Lembit's sword, Estonia will survive. Not only survive, but more importantly be free.

Our problem is that Lembit's sword was not in our hands for 700 years. We believe it was taken from his dead body by Otto von Mentzenkampf, one of the original Brothers of the Sword who may well be the man who killed him. No one knew what happened to the sword afterwards, until an Estonian gardener digging in a far corner of the Mentzenkampf estate in 1918 discovered a lead-lined box containing a sword and some human bones.

Think of that: <u>Estonia was a vassal state occupied by foreigners for seven centuries. "Then we suddenly get our freedom in 1918. Why? It should be obvious, but let me tell you. The sword reappeared!</u>

The gardener liked the look of the sword and decided to keep it, but he brought the box of bones to the German pastor of Suure-Jaani, a man called Merkel, who gave it a quick look and had it reburied in the potter's field beside the cemetery. About 20 years later, the next pastor, another German named Rosenkranz who had an interest in the history of the parish, discovered Merkel's notes about the reburial in the parish register and, being curious, had the box dug up. He was intrigued by a faded inscription on the box, just one word: "Lambite," which we know was the name used by the chronicler Henry of Livonia for Lembit. Rosenkranz questioned the gardener and learned about the existence of the sword. He told the gardener he had no business keeping the sword and reclaimed it for the Mentzenkampf family.

I can anticipate your thoughts. <u>Yes, that was in 1939, when Estonia again lost her freedom.</u>

The count at that time had no sense of history. For him the sword was of no importance and he stuffed it away somewhere in his mansion. There the matter would have remained, except that his son saw it one day and, being curious, did some research and pieced together its history. Sulev, who occasionally did part-time work for the Mentzenkampfs, overheard him telling another German count about the sword, and he immediately told me.

We knew that, because of the Molotov-Ribbentrop pact, the Germans would be leaving Estonia shortly. What was I supposed to do? It was clear to me that I had somehow been chosen to reclaim the sword for Estonia. So I got Sulev to help me break into the manor one night. Unfortunately, we couldn't find the sword and we were almost caught, except that Sulev had the wit to set a fire as a diversion. We got away but the place burned down. Anyway, we were too late; the sword must have already been shipped to Germany.

The story could have ended there, except for the man who showed up in your church. We knew you were being targeted by the Reds and some of my scouts had already noticed him skulking around the church and your manse. We were afraid he might be a Red assassin, so when one of my boys got an anonymous message that you were in danger that Sunday, there was no time to do anything but go to the church and be ready to stop him.

As Juhan told you, the lads made their presence known to him, so nothing did happen. I was waiting outside and followed him a couple of kilometers into the woods, where he had been hiding. I wanted to see what he was up to, so I ambushed him and tied him up, intending to put the fear of God in him before sending him packing. He told me he was not a Russian commie, but of half-Estonian blood from near the Latvian border and had once worked for a Baltic baron. I was curious. Why was he spying on you? Why would he want to shoot you?

He wouldn't tell me, so I threatened to cut off one of his fingers if he didn't answer me. He mustn't have believed me or else he was tougher than I thought, so I had no choice. After I cut off his little finger he told me that he wasn't planning to shoot you; *he was just looking for Lembit's sword*. Well, that got my attention. I had to prod him some more, but eventually he told me that a silversmith he knew told him the sword was worth a lot of money. According to him it was still somewhere in this area.

I knew that if Lembit's sword was still in Estonia, I had to find it, and I was ready to do anything to recover it.

To make a long story short, he told me that after he lost his job, he had started to break into places and sell his loot to a crooked silversmith in Viljandi. He was the one who told the man that one of Count von Mentzenkampf's servants had offered to sell him a valuable sword that he claimed had belonged to Lembit. The silversmith wanted the sword but the price was too high. He told the robber that if he could steal the sword from the servant, they would both be rich men.

The robber did some checking and learned that the only servant who still lived in the area was Jüri Reimann, and that it had been Reimann's father who had first found the sword. He was convinced that he had found his man. The only problem was that Jüri had died recently. Since your wife had inherited his farm, he thought that you, Pastor, had to know where the sword was. Someone had even told him that you had been seen one night carrying a long bundle that you were trying to hide, so he wanted to know where you had hidden it. That's why he was spying on you.

The man must have seen how excited I was by all this and figured out that I had no intention of letting him go. He tried to escape and I had to stab him several times to stop him. Later, I got Sulev to help me hide the body in a ditch near the Viljandi Road. I was going to ask you about the sword after we came back from this ambush, but if you are reading this then that obviously is no longer possible.

So this letter is my final effort to recover the sword for our country. No matter what it takes, we must get it back so that our people can rally around it to drive out our enemies. *You, Pastor, are now the chosen one, the only one who can do this. Do not fail your people. If you have the sword, or know its location, you MUST use it to rally our people. Moses had a staff with which he led his people to freedom. Well, Lembit's sword can do the same for us.* I believe that you, more than anyone else I know, will understand and appreciate the importance of what I am asking you to do. God bless you, Pastor.

> Toomas Sillaots
> Captain,
> First Vändra Brigade,
> Kaitseliit

Kingsepp frowned as he folded up the letter. He was appalled. Far be it for him to be judgmental, but he couldn't help but feel that Toomas, a murderer, and Sulev, who had abetted him, had met up with the hand of God. No one should be allowed to murder with impunity, no matter how great the cause. Their fate had been to reap what they themselves had sowed. God's justice had been done.

Still, he was beset by unsettling thoughts. Toomas had almost been reasonable when he was talking about the positive role his Taara faith had played in his life; but all the while he had been hiding a heinous crime – not that he saw it as a crime, if his letter was to be taken at face value.

The German crusader knights, too, had indiscriminately slaughtered his Estonian forefathers in the name of God, and expected to be rewarded by heaven for their deeds. How different were those people from the Communists who were killing for what they thought was a higher cause? All those "isms" – religious dogmas and secular ideologies: patriotism, capitalism, communism, or whatever – often lost sight of true human values and ended up resembling each other. Were any of their so-called higher values worth more than people's lives?

The pastor didn't think so, and reminded himself of what his mentor, Prof. Kapp, had tried to imbue in his students after returning to Tartu with an enlightened approach to Christian theology. The two rocks on which Christianity was built, Kapp had told them, were love and forgiveness. Everything else was inconsequential window dressing.

Jesus, Kapp had explained, had a powerful message, "But how seriously do you think people would have taken the words of a poor, barefoot itinerant preacher? That's why Paul and the other church fathers dressed up His message the way they did. And since then, for the past 2,000 years, people have felt free to distort and co-opt those teachings for all kinds of political purposes. Our job is to cut through the accumulated window dressing and get back to what Christ actually espoused."

Those words had persuaded Kingsepp to persevere in his projected career when he had had doubts, and they still served him well, especially now.

As for the sword, he dismissed it as a fairy tale that could only appeal to youngsters. Toomas might choose to believe it, but the pastor had always considered him to be somewhat immature, a fellow who spent much of his life among adolescents. How could anyone in his right mind commit murder because of a belief that the fate of Estonia was dependent on a sword that may not even be what he thought it was? There were perfectly solid geo-political reasons why Estonia was often a doormat for the great powers that surrounded it, and it would take a lot more than a mythical sword to solve its difficulties.

He had to admit, though, that he was curious about the connection with Jüri Reimann. Could it be that the mild-mannered, self-effacing man whose funeral he had conducted had stolen the sword? And what about Tädi? If Jüri indeed had stolen the sword from his employer, how could she not know that? It seemed impossible to believe, but could it be that her apparently straight-laced rectitude was a mask behind which lurked another person whom he had yet to meet? Were all those humorous tales about a silly German Count meant to cover a secret enmity for the Baltic Barons? Most of all, he wondered, did she know where the sword was?

He would have to sound her out on these points, the pastor thought. For the time being, however, there were certainly far more serious things to consider, now that it looked like the Reds were definitely on the run and the Germans were poised to take over. What would life be like under the new masters? Would they be any better off or merely under a different thumb?

Chapter Nineteen

The *metsavennad* knew all about the German advance from the Finnish news bulletins they were able to pick up on a short wave radio one of them had managed to spirit away from a Russian office. Many of them were tired of their spartan life in the woods and believed a German victory would allow them to disband and return to their homes. Anybody would be better than the Reds, they argued. Other forest brothers, however, argued that the Germans couldn't be trusted any more than the Russians, so it would be a mistake to disband. If any of them planned to go back to their homes, they should remain vigilant, and ready to take up arms again, if – or more likely, when – that became necessary.

Meanwhile, as soon as they heard that the Germans had crossed the border into Estonia, Zhukov and his gang left, followed closely by the Soviet teachers and other functionaries who had been imported to turn Estonia into a communist paradise. The withdrawal of the Russians from the village before the arrival of the Germans led to some momentary chaos. Strong emotions that had been bottled up for two years could not be contained any longer, and more than a few villagers seized the opportunity to settle grudges and take vigilante action against collaborators. *Kaitseliit* militia patrols eventually restored order, but not before some unfortunate incidents, including three revenge killings.

Among the victims was Randar Salu, the sexton's son, who had hoped to benefit from the new classless society the Reds had promised. Because he had helped to pull down the obelisk commemorating the War of Independence, some of the youths who had gathered the broken pieces and hidden them in the woods, cornered Randar one night and beat him senseless. They only wanted to teach him a lesson, they later said, but the young man died from his injuries a week later. His father was heartbroken but, as a patriot himself, found it hard to blame the youths. "I could see this coming," he told the pastor. "I warned Randar not to get mixed up with the Reds, but he wouldn't listen to me."

The lightning strike of the German forces meant that the last of the Red units to leave had no easy escape route and had to fight for their lives. German warplanes even flew sorties over the area, in some instances setting the woods on fire with incendiary bombs. Several farms were destroyed in that way, and bomb craters dotted quite a few hayfields. In desperation, the Russians dropped paratroopers behind the German lines to help their comrades, and in some cases were able to mount effective rearguard actions. Even after the Germans seized full control of Estonia, Red paratroopers continued to be sent occasionally to harass the Germans behind their lines. Estonian home guard units were often the ones who had to track those paratroopers down.

When the German army units rolled into the village, they were welcomed by many as liberators, but the honeymoon lost its luster quickly. The "free elections" the Germans had promised the village council turned out to be illusory, since it soon became apparent that the councillors' freedom to act was rigidly controlled by the Germans' regional high command. Then the councillors noticed one morning that the portraits of Päts, Laidoner and Tõnisson, which had been rehung in the council offices, had been replaced again, this time by a large picture of Adolf Hitler.

Still, most of the parish considered that their lives had improved since the Russians had been driven out. The confiscated farms, including the church farm, were returned to the owners. The secondary school re-opened with most of the old teachers returning, and the Russian-imposed restrictions on religious practice were lifted. For the pastor, these were welcome changes, and he was quick to reconvene his Confirmation class and his Bible study groups. Best of all, he thought, Peeter Kallas reappeared in church one Sunday and told him he was ready to rejoin the church council, if he would be welcome after his resignation. Kingsepp said quickly. "It's not a problem. We all understand the pressure you were under. I think I can speak for everyone when I say that. And Mr. Männik and I will be more than pleased to have you back as the chairman. He's as dutiful as ever, but I think that at his age he's found that being chairman is more of a burden than it used to be."

"One other thing," Peeter said. "Siiman also wants to rejoin the council, but I don't think Andrus will be coming back. He was really shaken by the confrontation with Zhukov and says his nerves are still shot. I would suggest we don't bother him, at least for the time being."

"I agree. We all got a fright from those ruffians, but you're probably right that he took it harder than most of us. A bit of time off might help him get back on track. But, what about you? You must have had a hard time of it here while some of us were in the woods."

"It was no picnic, but at least I got to sleep in my own bed and eat proper food," Peeter replied, looking at the pastor somewhat apprehensively. "I know it must seem funny that they allowed me to do that after Zhukov told me that he considered me a public enemy, but they had their reasons, as you'll see. Still, for a long time after I resigned from the church council, I went through a period of great anxiety. As the manager of the linen factory, I knew I was one of the "parasites" that they wanted to get rid of, so I was constantly in fear of being arrested. I was even getting ready to join you fellows in the woods."

"So why didn't you?" the pastor prompted, his curiosity aroused.

"It was due to that awful man Kivisik," Peeter said. "I say awful and I mean it, but he probably saved my life. He came to see me soon after Zhukov threatened me and said that if I did what he asked me to do, he would make sure that I wasn't arrested."

"Kivisik, eh? the pastor said. "You know that I also made a deal with him that I think saved the lives of at least twenty people, myself included. Of course it probably saved his life too."

"I heard about that," Peeter said. "It was the same kind of thing with me. It was clear that the only reason Kivisik wanted to protect me was self-interest. He had come up with quite a clever plan. Since I was the only person locally who knew how to operate the plant, he would convince Zhukov that I should continue to do that, but I would be listed as an ordinary member of a new workers management committee. That way Zhukov would look good to Moscow as a commissar who was able to keep up production while establishing the new order.

"To make it look legitimate, Kivisik told me I would have to drop all bourgeois activities, including going to church. I didn't want to do that, of course, but he said I had no choice. The alternative was to be sent to Siberia, together with my wife and daughter. What could I do? If it was only me, I might have resisted, but I couldn't jeopardize my family. I had to agree."

"I don't think that was wrong of you," the pastor said. "Kivisik knows how to put people over a barrel and we know how ruthless he can be. But I'm curious, what was in it for him?"

"That's the tricky part. As the only person who knew what was really going on in the factory, I would be able to rig the books so that Kivisik could skim off ten percent of everything we took in. I've always been a stickler for honesty, but again I had no choice. And I'm sorry to say that part of me didn't mind stealing from the Communists. If the proceeds had gone anywhere but to that thief Kivisik, I wouldn't have minded at all."

"I don't think you have to worry about breaking any commandments in this case," the pastor said with a smile. "After all that we've seen and been through these past years, I can no longer believe that ethical rules are categorical. The Greeks may have got it right when they said we have to consider the results of our actions as well as our intentions and the actions themselves. How could you possibly jeopardize your family's lives by scrupulously following a rigid rule? The God I believe in would understand why you did what you did."

"Thank you for saying that, Pastor. I did have qualms, as I mentioned, but that's what I believe too. Anyway, for better or for worse, that's what I did, and Kivisik, I can say that much for him, upheld his part of the deal. I don't think Zhukov ever trusted me, but he was being commended by Moscow for the profitable way he kept the linen factory running with what it believed was a worker's management committee."

"You know, of course, that the other linen factory was closed down," Peeter said after a brief pause. "Zhukov tried to do the same thing with it, expropriating it for the state and setting up a workers management committee there also. But they were unable to keep it going."

"Why was that?" the pastor asked.

"Well, we were a strictly local concern, with local shareholders, all of whom lost their holdings, of course. But none of us left. The key difference was that the other company was Swedish-owned and had a Swedish manager. As soon as the factory was expropriated, the Swedish manager and all of his key employees went back to Sweden. So Zhukov ended up trying to run a pretty intricate factory with inexperienced people, none of whom really knew how to do it. I mean their new operations person had never done anything but tend one minor machine, and the others were even less experienced.

"Zhukov managed to cover up that failure by telling Moscow that a second factory wasn't viable here, so he would dismantle the second plant and ship it to Russia where it could be better used. He also arrested seven of the Estonian workers during the round-up of so-called subversives. He said they were shirking their duties and needed some re-education in Siberia. But it seems they ended up going to Russia to help set up and work in the dismantled factory. I think he got another commendation for that initiative," Peeter said with an inadvertent snort.

"Anyway, our biggest problem arose after Stalin began his scorched earth policy to delay the Germans. Zhukov immediately ordered us to dismantle all our machines so they could be packed off to Russia. That's when I had my big idea."

"Every night, after the workers who had been taking things apart left, two trusted workers and I would go back and sabotage their efforts. That's not hard to do if you know the business. For example, we would strip the threads on bolts so that they couldn't be unscrewed, or fill up vats and tanks with noxious chemicals so that they would have to be laboriously emptied and cleaned.

"It was like Scheherazade in the story of *The Arabian Nights*; we succeeded in delaying things, maybe not for a thousand nights, but sufficiently, as it turned out.

Because we were so slow, Zhukov arranged for a destruction battalion to help us. I knew exactly when they were supposed to arrive, so I was able to alert the *metsavennad*. I think you know what happened next, Pastor."

"Wait a minute," the pastor said. "Are you saying that it was you who told the *metsavennad* the time they set up the ambush at

Ojasilla? You know that I was in that group? I didn't go to Ojasilla, however, because only a few experienced fighters went with the explosives expert. But the Reds never showed up...."

"I know," Peeter interrupted. "They were delayed by some engine troubles, so they decided to take a shorter route. But your group did a pretty effective job because the destruction battalion never made it to the factory."

"So that's why you still have a factory to manage," the pastor said. "We did see some fighting the next day, however, at Kavasoo," he added after a pause. The pastor stared into the distance for a moment before shaking his head. "Three of our men were killed there, you know, and maybe six or seven of the Reds."

Chapter Twenty

Although the pastor had never had to fire his rifle during his six weeks in the woods, the suffering he had witnessed remained etched in his mind – the young men whose lives he had seen snuffed out, the maimed bodies of the wounded, and the mangled corpses of the victims of the terror squads, which he had buried after his group had found them in burned-out farmhouses. He looked different, Evely had told him, not just because of his gauntness, but because he was so somber and often seemed lost in thought, staring into the distance. "You never smile any more," she told him one day. "I know it must have been difficult, but you have to put all that behind you and think of the future, for the children's sake." It was good advice, the kind he himself might have dispensed six weeks ago. But no matter how hard he tried, he couldn't control his moods. For the first time, he began to understand how unconsoling the bromides of friends, however well-intentioned, could be to those who were suffering. He resolved to do better, to try to really connect with his parishioners. He hoped that, by sharing with them his own feelings, they would together regain their faith in humanity and find the closure they were seeking.

That was why on a sunny Saturday morning, a couple of weeks after returning from the woods, he found himself riding out to the Eidepere farm. He didn't expect it to be an easy visit, but it was something he felt he had to do. Oskar and Jutta Eidepere were the parents of Sulev, the young forest brother who had aided and abetted Toomas Sillaots in his clandestine activities before being murdered by a Red terror squad. The pastor had reflected for a long time on how much he should tell the parents about Sulev's activities and had finally decided that whatever Sulev had done was between him and his Maker. No purpose would be served by giving the parents another cross to bear. If anything, they deserved to hear something positive from him about their only son's last days.

In reaching this decision he was mindful that Sulev's father, Oskar, was not a well man after suffering a serious accident a month ago, roughly around the time his son had been killed. Oskar had been ordered by the Reds to join a work gang repairing a bombed-out bridge abutment and had been loading a cart with field stones when an axle broke and the load shifted. A large boulder had slid off the cart, badly crushing Oskar's right leg, which had had to be amputated just below the knee. In falling he had also hit his head against another rock, causing a debilitating concussion.

Oskar had been a friendly, always-ready-to-help kind of man who had once served on the church council. Now, apparently, he had become morose and uncommunicative. Since his release from the hospital he had spent his days sitting in his kitchen muttering to himself, chain-smoking and staring at the wall. He never wanted to see any visitors and told his wife to send away even his oldest friends. When a few of them insisted on seeing him, he had become angry and hurled curses at the visitors until they retreated.

The first thing the pastor noticed as he approached the Eidepere farm was how rundown it had become. The neat farmyard he remembered was now overgrown with weeds, and the moss on the roof shingles and the flaking paint of the farmhouse gave it the appearance of a derelict dwelling. A red-eyed, haggard-looking Jutta Eidepere met him in the yard after he had turned in at the gate. "Hello Pastor," she hailed him. "I'm sorry to say this, but if you're here to see Oskar, I don't think this is a good time."

"Now Jutta, you don't have to be polite with me," the pastor said. "From what I hear, there is never a good time for him. But I think the words of our Lord can be comforting at any time. I think he might like to hear what I have to say about Sulev. You know that I was there for his burial."

"I heard that you were there, Pastor, and I want to thank you for that. He had been spending too much time with that Sillaots fellow and I was afraid he wouldn't get a proper Christian burial. I could never understand what he saw in Taara. Whatever it was, he didn't get it from us. We're good Christians."

"I know that, and I'm glad to hear you say it," the pastor said. "I don't think that underneath it all Sulev was any different. He may have got caught up in other things when he was in the woods, but

124

he was probably influenced by some of the people he was associating with. I don't think that Toomas Sillaots was the best person to be in charge of impressionable young men. How did Sulev get to join up with him, anyway?"

"It was just Scouts at first, "Jutta said, "which we encouraged. But then Sillaots started painting rosy pictures for the boys about the golden age before the German conquest. That was the start of the Taara business, and before we knew it, the boys were running around spying on everyone, shooting off guns at the rifle range and God knows what else. I thought it was too much for 17-year-olds to handle, but Sulev loved it and we couldn't keep him away."

"No one can blame you or Oskar for anything," the pastor said. "And you don't have to worry about Sulev. I believe he was a good lad at heart and I made sure that he was sent to meet his Maker with a Christian prayer."

He could see that his words had had a calming effect on her. "Maybe you should tell Oskar that," she said. "He's so bitter and angry at the Russians that he can't think of anything else. I'll leave you two alone," she said after opening the farmhouse door for him.

As the pastor's eyes adjusted to the dim light inside, he saw Oskar dozing in a chair beside the hearth. He sat in another chair a couple of meters away and waited for the invalid to awake. It didn't take long. Oskar stirred, looked around, noticed the pastor and harrumphed, "Go home, Pastor," he said. "I don't want to talk to you."

"That's okay," the pastor responded. "But I think I'll just sit here for a while before I go – if you don't mind, that is."

Oskar gave him an angry look. "No, I guess not, as long as you don't preach to me. I've put all that behind me. God has done nothing for me and I've no interest in Him any more. All I want to do is to kill Russians, as many as possible. I'd do it myself, but look at me; good for nothing and whose fault? Theirs! And they killed my son, my only son. What have I got to live for now?"

Oskar's shoulders heaved and his body shook convulsively. Anger, anguish and self-pity were all written on his face. From what the pastor had heard, the few people he saw indulged him, overlooking his outbursts and treating him with kid gloves. That only reinforced his unruly behavior, the pastor thought, and after a minute's reflection, he decided to take a different tack.

"You asked me what you have to live for. You've got Jutta," he said. "She also is in great pain and needs your support to overcome it. Instead, you're ignoring her as if you're the only person who is suffering. Why are you so selfish? Don't you think you should try to help the woman who has given you the best years of her life for more than thirty years? When was the last time you really talked to her? Why don't you hold her hand tonight and ask her what's on her mind? You can be a great help to each other."

He could see that Oskar had primed himself to shout him down, but that gradually his anger had subsided. Now he stared quietly at the pastor. After a few minutes, he said. "You're right, Pastor. I do owe her a lot."

Chapter Twenty-One

As soon as he could, Kingsepp took two days off to move back all the farm implements and livestock that had been hidden from the Reds at Metsa Talu. Restoring the church farm to its former condition, however, was going to take much longer, he thought, wondering if the parish funds would even be up to it. The model dairy barn was a charred mess, having been set on fire by one of the retreating "destruction battalions." What was left of the herd was in a dire condition; some of the best milkers had been slaughtered for beef, and many of the others had dried up in the absence of regular milking. The horses that once had been so sleek had become scrawny and weak from neglect. Nothing but weeds could be seen on the fields.

"So much for the workers' paradise," thought the pastor as he surveyed the farm with Jukku, who seemed happy enough to have the pastor back in charge, even though it had meant giving up the ten hectares the communists had assigned to him. He merely smiled and nodded when the pastor told him, "We won't be harvesting much this year. But we can try to get things ready for next summer by plowing the fields."

As they approached one of the back fields, they saw Eero Oder, the new village reeve, walking out to meet them. The pastor liked Oder, who was a cousin of the church council's treasurer, and was glad that he had been persuaded to take up the position of reeve. Oder had been reluctant after having been dismissed by the Russians from his previous post as the village bookkeeper. He had also ended up on Zhukov's list and had spent nearly two months in the woods. After that, he had thought it best to keep a low profile, but then he had been prevailed upon by his forest brother friends. "There's no one else with any experience left to do the job," they told him.

"Your wife told me I'd find you here," Oder said after greeting the pastor. "I see that things look just as bad as I was told, maybe worse. But don't worry. We're setting up special work groups to help restore the ruined farms, beginning with the worst cases. We would like to start here next week, if that suits you. We still have the plans for the barn, so it will end up looking pretty much the same."

Heartened by the rebuilding plan for the farm, the pastor was in a good mood at supper that night. After the cold sausage, hard cheese and stale rye bread that had been their usual fare in the woods, the pork roast and sauerkraut tasted delicious. He was savoring every mouthful. Evely and Tädi were eating even more slowly, but for a different reason. Each was feeding a child and could manage only an occasional forkful of their own while coaxing the children to take "one more bite."

"It's good to be together again," Kingsepp said expansively to no one in particular, as he reached for his cigarettes after cleaning off his plate. As he lit up, Evely took the children away to wash their hands and chins. After a few puffs, the pastor caught Tädi's eye. "There's something I've been meaning to ask you. I was told that your Jüri's father once found an old sword in a field on Count von Mentzenkampf's estate. You wouldn't know anything about that, would you?"

Tädi looked puzzled. "No, he never said anything to me about that. It may have been before my time. Jüri grew up on the estate, you know. Why do you ask?"

"No particular reason," the pastor answered. "It's just something someone said and I was curious. That's all."

"Well, if it's a sword you're interested in, I remember that Jüri once pointed one out to me hanging above a fireplace in the manor house. It was very old, he told me, but he never suggested his father had found it. Maybe that's the one your fellow was thinking about."

"That could be," the pastor said after a minute's reflection. "I'll keep that in mind in case the subject comes up again. You wouldn't know where that sword is now, would you?"

"No. Probably in Germany. The Mentzenkampfs packed everything except some of the older furniture when they left. And then the place burned down, of course. So your guess is as good as mine."

Just as I thought, the pastor said to himself. *She really doesn't know anything about this. It's a dead end or else a shaggy dog story. Sad, though, that it led to Toomas murdering that fellow. Just as well I didn't tell her that part of the story.*

Later that night as Karl and Evely were getting ready for bed, Evely said to him. "Tädi said you're interested in an old sword that the Mentzenkampfs had. I once saw a photograph of the old Count standing in front of the fireplace in what looks like his sitting room, and there was a sword hanging on the wall behind him. If you are still interested, I could look for the picture next time we're out at Metsa Talu."

A week later, while working in the rectory office, he was surprised to find Mr. Oder knocking on his door.

"I wouldn't be troubling you, Pastor, but this looks like it could be important. A message came in over the telephone that Major Heinrich Hauptmann in Paide town wants to see you as soon as possible. He's not someone we would want to offend, I've been told, so I've organized a car for you tomorrow morning, if that suits you."

Sitting in the German officers' staff room in Paide the following morning, Kingsepp still couldn't think of a reason why a German officer would want to speak to him, particularly someone like Major Hauptmann, who, Mr. Oder had told him, was in charge of the military police and counter-terrorism over much of the territory east of Vändra. He didn't have long to ponder that question; within a few minutes, a very smart-looking officer of about 35 was clicking his heels in front of him.

"Pastor Kingsepp, I presume," he said with a smile. "I'm told you learned German at university and speak it very well, so would it be all right if we carried on in the language of Goethe and Schiller?" At the pastor's affirmative nod, he continued, "I'm delighted you were able to come so quickly. I trust things in Vändra are much better now."

"Yes, thank you. Things are much better."

Hauptmann again flashed a smile. "That's what we like to hear. But I am sure you would like to know why I wanted to see you. We've had a very interesting case come up here...well, actually in

129

Järva-Madise down the road a bit. Your forest brothers there put up a fierce resistance to the Reds, which was a big help to us. But after it was over, they came to us with a prisoner. Rather curiously, this man had been fighting alongside them, and by their own accounts he had been an effective rifleman. But a witness had sworn he had once seen this man in a Red uniform in Vändra. They wanted to shoot him, but he convinced them that they should talk to me first.

"I was intrigued and agreed to see him. His story was that he was really an anti-communist Estonian patriot who had been forced to work for the Reds as an interpreter. He said that if we asked you, you would vouch that he had worked under cover for the Estonians. Naturally, I had him checked out, but he had been using several different names. One of the names he gave us matched that of an Estonian interpreter in Vändra. You, of course, are the parish pastor in Vändra, so you should know if he is telling the truth."

The pastor's heart sank. He knew exactly what was coming next. Hauptmann again flashed a smile. "He says he is really Karl Kivisik. Is that true? Is he an Estonian patriot or is he a Red?"

Kingsepp felt flustered but tried not to show it. The reappearance of Karl Kivisik was the last thing he had expected today. The man had disappeared almost immediately after he had handed over Zhukov's list to Kingsepp. No one in Vändra had heard of him since, and the pastor had given up thinking that he would actually have to fulfill his promise to vouch for him to the Nazis. Now, he might be holding the power of life or death over Kivisik. And what exactly had Kivisik told Hauptmann? Would he himself be compromised? He really needed some time to reflect on his response. Meanwhile, Hauptmann was still smiling at him expectantly.

"I...er...it's a complex issue," he finally managed to say. "There was a man named Karl Kivisik who was an interpreter for the Reds in Vändra. If your man is indeed the Karl Kivisik I knew, then, yes, he did help me and some other Estonians by..."

"It's all right, Pastor," Hauptmann broke in, still smiling. "You don't have to spell it out. All I wanted to know is whether this man was a Red. Thank you for your help. You can go back to Vändra now; Lieutenant Eisner will tell your driver you're ready."

On the drive back, Kingsepp was silent, reflecting on what had just happened. Major Hauptmann had not given anything away. Behind all those smiles and the heel-clicking politeness, he had sensed an alert intelligence. Hauptmann, he noticed, had registered his use of the past tense when he said he had known Kivisik. Other than that, nothing. Would his association with Kivisik cause him to come under suspicion? Would he be placed under observation? He'd had enough of that under the Reds. Damn that Kivisik anyway.

He was immediately sorry for thinking that. For all he knew, Hauptmann might have already had Kivisik shot. And if not yet, maybe soon, doomed by his mealy-mouthed hesitancy to vouch for him. He had promised to do that, so why had he obfuscated? He should go back and set things straight.

But when he asked the driver to do that, the driver refused. There wasn't enough time. He only had the car for another hour. Besides, it probably wouldn't be possible to see the major again without an appointment. Kingsepp resolved to telephone Hauptmann as soon as they got back.

Mr. Oder was kind enough to let him use his office phone, since Kingsepp's own line had not yet been repaired. It was easier to get through than he had anticipated. Hauptmann sounded friendly, even after the pastor said he was concerned about Kivisik's fate, but he stopped him after only a few words.

"Don't worry, Pastor. We won't have to bother you again. We know what kind of a person you are. And we already know everything we need to know about this man. Goodbye, Pastor."

Kingsepp soon found himself immersed in other affairs. Busy with the parish work that had been left undone during his time in the woods, the repairs to the farm buildings, and his family commitments, he often forgot about Kivisik. Whatever happened to him now was up to Kivisik himself, the pastor rationalized. He had done what he had promised. But sometimes late at night, when he couldn't fall asleep, he felt uneasy. Had he done the right thing? Should he have done more? What actually had happened to Kivisik?

Chapter Twenty-Two

Ever since his student days, whenever he felt stressed, Kingsepp would invariably reach for a cigarette. He had tried several times to kick the habit, but within days would always find an excuse to light up again. Even his time in the woods, when smoking was strictly forbidden, hadn't had a lasting effect. To make smoking a little harder for himself, he had recently started to buy his cigarettes, a few at a time, from a little shop he had rediscovered at the far end of the village. The shop was almost two kilometers from the manse, so even if he continued to smoke, at least the walk would do him good.

It wasn't really a tobacconist's shop, but a second-hand clothing emporium with several sidelines, notably tobacco products and "previously-owned" books. Racks of used clothing and shoes filled the front of the shop, with a narrow aisle leading to the wall of sturdy, unpainted shelves in the back where the shopkeeper kept the tobacco and books, as well as some curios. Despite the dust that coated most items, the pastor found the place interesting and sometimes spent fifteen minutes or more browsing before trekking back home.

After two or three visits, the main attraction for him became the shopkeeper. Avraham Mandelbaum, the only Jew left in the parish, was a good-natured, garrulous man of about 60, with whom the pastor enjoyed chatting. They were renewing a brief acquaintance that dated back almost five years to when Leah, Mandelbaum's wife, had died. At that time, the pastor had been in the rectory one evening when he heard a light tapping on the door. He was quite taken aback by the bushy-haired, big-bearded man who stood there, hat in hand, looking rueful.

"I have come, Pastor, to ask a favor of you, man to man," the man said. "I am not a member of your congregation, but my wife has just died and I would like you to say a prayer when I bury her."

"But you are not a Christian," the pastor interrupted.

"Very perceptive, Pastor. It is true that I am not a Christian. I am a Jew. But we share the same God and if I am not mistaken, your prophet Jesus was Yeshua, a Jew. Our Torah and your Bible have much in common, including many prayers that were familiar to my wife.

"I know you find this very curious; but I am not trying to mock you or be blasphemous. I am here because there is no Rabbi within a hundred kilometers. My Leah, God bless her, was a true believer, and she would rest more easily in her grave if a man of God said a prayer for her. Can you do this for her?"

Kingsepp, who had been gazing intently at the man as he spoke, was touched by his words. "I can see that you are a serious man," he said after a moment of reflection, "and are asking me out of love for your wife. I cannot refuse such a request."

That was how their relationship began, at a funeral for Mandelbaum's wife, attended by just the two of them. Mandelbaum had dug the grave himself, on a hillside in a forested area outside the village. Afterwards, the two men had returned to his little apartment behind the store to drink tea and eat egg salad sandwiches. After half an hour of awkward conversation, Kingsepp said goodbye and left, with no intention of ever returning. It was nearly four years later and only when he was contemplating a longer walk to buy cigarettes, that he remembered Mandelbaum's shop, tucked around a side street at the far end of the village.

Mandelbaum had been pleased to see him enter his shop again, and had insisted on preparing tea for the pastor. "I haven't forgotten the *mitzvah* you did for me, Pastor. You will always be welcome here."

More visits followed, and gradually the conversation of the two men changed from perfunctory to deeply personal, each of them speaking from the heart. One subject, however, seemed to be touchy. "You have never told me about your children," the pastor said on one of his early visits.

"They are in Riga. They have their life and I have mine," Mandelbaum answered, before changing the subject.

Later as they got to know each other better, Mandelbaum told the pastor that he was estranged from his children because they had become devoutly orthodox in their beliefs and he had steadfastly remained non-practicing, an atheist, if truth be told. "But they still pray for me," he said.

"Well, so will I," the pastor had responded. As the friendship between this odd pair developed, Kingsepp took to visiting the shop two or three times a month, even if he didn't need cigarettes. Instead, he would look over the books, many of which were philosophical in nature, before buying one. To his great delight, when he once bought a work by Dostoevsky, Mandelbaum confessed that he too was a devotee of that author. After that, as soon as Mandelbaum saw him coming, he would put the kettle on and prepare two cups of tea in the Russian style, in a delicate glass mug in a silver holder, with lots of sugar and a slice of lemon. The talk would follow after the first few sips.

The pastor's curiosity often made him steer the conversation to religious topics. He particularly wanted to know why Mandelbaum called himself an atheist. "All you have to do is look around," the older man answered. "Look at what the Russians and Germans have done to the Estonian people. We are being treated like cattle, shipped off to Siberia or murdered. Every day there are new examples of barbarism. When I see such things, how can I believe in God? I cannot comprehend how He could stand by and not do anything, if He exists, that is."

The pastor, who had met up with similar views before, always found such challenges to his belief stimulating. When he had been studying theology at Tartu, he had vowed to himself that if his faith couldn't withstand scrutiny, he would quit the ministry. But after three or four years of full-time ministry he had had to admit that his faith was slipping into a comfortable routine. He still believed, but in a complacent kind of way. Then the Soviet occupation woke him up. Suddenly, palpable evil stalked the land, and he, like everyone else, had to deal with it.

It wasn't God who was evil or uncaring; people were, he told Mandelbaum. People were often selfish and vindictive and acted ruthlessly towards each other. "That's what original sin means," he added. "We are not perfect, we need the grace of God to save us from ourselves. He showed us the way by sacrificing his Son.

135

There's no greater love than that; that's the example we have to follow."

These discussions invigorated Kingsepp, though he could never get Mandelbaum to agree with him. "Original sin is an insult to the human race," Mandelbaum had once told him. "There may be a lot of evil people, but not because of original sin. And it's not God's grace that makes us good. What I believe is that we are all capable of every type of behavior, and the difference between good and evil comes from education and socialization. The Bible is not the only source of wisdom, you know. You should read some of the modern theories of mind, Freud for example. But he's a Jew, so you probably haven't heard of him," he added half-jokingly.

The most the older man would concede was that religion could benefit some people. Most people aren't educated enough to think for themselves, so they are like children, he said. They'll try to be good because they fear punishment or they expect a reward. "That's what Heaven and Hell are all about, and for them God is the strict parent who enforces the rules."

"But I consider that a primitive kind of morality, only suitable for illiterate or uneducated people," Mandelbaum said. "We have to progress beyond that stage. We can't really call ourselves intelligent unless we have morality within ourselves. We don't need an external God; we need to find God in ourselves. That's how I interpret what Nietzsche said about God being dead, but of course that's not how Stalin and Hitler and others have interpreted it."

Jesus's approach to morality, especially his Golden Rule, was not all that different from Mandelbaum's views, the pastor thought when he had reflected on these conversations during his time in the woods. He looked forward to continuing the discussion.

One afternoon, in the early days of the German occupation, he was on his way to the shop when he was horrified to see a large yellow Star of David in the window. It had been several years now that he had stopped thinking of Mandelbaum as a Jew.

"What's that all about?" he asked, pointing at the yellow star as he opened the door to the shop. "You're becoming religious finally, are you?" The moment his words slipped out he was sorry. This was no laughing matter. But Mandelbaum didn't mind, countering with his own joke.

"Well, sort of," Mandelbaum replied. "But it's not up to me. It's the law now. All Jewish establishments have to step up their advertising."

"And what do the rest of us have to post?" said the pastor. He knew full well that nothing good, only bad, followed from such laws. Why else would anyone have to be differentiated from others? It was what farmers did when they were culling their herds.

Without another word, he angrily ripped the yellow star from the window and tore it into shreds. "You don't need that," he said when he was done. "Everyone knows you are the only Jew in the village."

"I wish you hadn't done that," Mandelbaum said. "It won't change anything; it will only make more trouble."

"You haven't done anything wrong. But if anyone complains, send them to me. I'll set them straight."

No one did go to the pastor to complain. He heard nothing further about yellow stars until three weeks later, when he again went to Mandelbaum's shop. There it was again, the yellow star, back in the window. Kingsepp tore it off before entering the shop, where, instead of moving forward to welcome him, Mandelbaum remained seated in the back where the light was dimmer. As Kingsepp approached his chair, Mandelbaum turned to look at him squarely and said sadly, "I told you nothing good would come of your taking down the star." His face, the pastor now saw, was puffed up and black and blue, and his right arm was in a sling. "I'm sorry I won't be able to offer you tea today."

"Oh God!" the pastor exclaimed. "What have they done to you? I'm so sorry. So very sorry! Let me make the tea. I'm sure you could use a cup." After all the times he had watched Mandelbaum prepare the tea, he knew exactly how it was done, and it didn't take him long. When they had each had their customary first sip in silence, the pastor insisted that Mandelbaum tell him everything. "I want to know so I can lodge a complaint."

"Thank you Pastor, but no thank you. I really don't want your help. It won't do any good with these thugs. And the more attention that's paid to me, the more I'm going to suffer. This is not random violence; it's part of their program. Haven't you been following the news? They just don't like Jews. I'd get out of here, if I could; but it's too late for me now. Anyway there's no place I can go. I guess I'll go down in history as the last Jew in Vändra."

"But you're not even a real Jew; you're an atheist."

"Well, that's two strikes against me. How do you think it would look? A Lutheran pastor going to the defense of a Jewish atheist? You'd be defrocked before you know it and riding the rails with me to a concentration camp."

Despite the banter, both were conscious of the seriousness of the situation. Kingsepp didn't push the issue any further, but he vowed to himself to go see Lieutenant Werner Klapp, the officer in charge of the small military contingent in Vändra. Klapp was an earnest young man of thirty or so who seemed to be a practicing Christian. At least he had started off attending services but had not been seen in the church for the past several weeks.

Klapp didn't seem surprised when the pastor called on him in the house commandeered by the soldiers for their barracks. "Hello, Pastor. I thought you might be coming around. I haven't given up on you, but it's been busy lately. I do intend to attend services again when things are quieter."

"That's good of you. I'll look forward to seeing you in church again, but..."

"Oh, you will," the young soldier broke in somewhat nervously, "and very soon, I promise. I find it helps me practice my Estonian, I mean in addition to the other things ... the religious aspect."

"Actually, Lieutenant, that's not what I came about. There's something else I want to discuss with you, something much more serious – something that we as Christians should not tolerate."

The lieutenant's eyes narrowed. "If it's what I think it is, Pastor," he interjected, "I don't really want to discuss it. It's out of my hands. I have to follow orders. There's nothing I can do."

Kingsepp felt himself getting angry, but tried to speak calmly. "You do call yourself a Christian, don't you?"

He waited for Klapp's nod.

"Well, if you truly want to follow Christ then you can't treat a fellow human being so callously. You really need to consider very seriously whether you want to follow orders or save your immortal soul. You do have a choice you know. And remember, when it comes to standing before your Maker in your final hour, He's not going to judge you by how well you followed orders; He's going to ask you how you treated your fellow man."

"Pastor, you can't know the kind of pressure I face. I already tried to follow the golden rule. I really did, you know, and look where it got me. One more misstep and I'll be treated like one of them. So don't ask me to do it again."

"What do you mean?" the pastor asked.

"I mean that I didn't report you for tearing down the old Jew's star. But some of my own men are real Nazis, so word got back to Major Hauptmann anyway, and I had to go to headquarters to explain myself. He called it a refresher course, but it was really house arrest for two weeks. If it happens again I'm finished. He didn't spell it out like that, but he didn't need to. He'll be watching me, he said. And then you had to go and do it again."

"Oh, I had no idea."

"Well, don't worry. I didn't report you. I told the *Sturmbannführer* the old Jew had done it himself this time."

"Oh no, that's even worse," the pastor said. "His blood will be on my hands. I can't let that happen; I'll have to explain to the major that it was all a mistake."

"I don't mean to be disrespectful, but don't waste your breath, Pastor," Klapp said. "The old Jew's goose is cooked anyway. It's just a matter of time."

The pastor was shocked. "And you're OK with that?"

"No Pastor, I'm not. I am not a Nazi. I joined the army to defend my country but it looks like one can't just be a patriot. I would like to follow Christ's teachings, not Hitler's, but no matter what you say, it can't be done. It's me or the Jew, or it could be you. The major is deadly serious about this. You know he's been involved in setting up some prison camps for Jews in southern Estonia. There aren't very many Jews here, so they're importing them from Latvia and Poland and God knows where. And you know, I hear they're not really prisons, but places where people are taken to be killed. We're all going to be damned for this... I don't know if I can bear this much longer."

He looked at the pastor with piteous eyes. A sob escaped his lips and his body trembled until with an excruciating effort he fought his way back to self-control. Kingsepp's heart went out to the distraught young man. There's a man heading for a serious breakdown, he thought. "I think this would be a good time to pray," he said, kneeling and clasping his hands. He waited for Klapp to join him before beginning: "Our Father...."

Half an hour later, Kingsepp was back in Mandelbaum's shop. "I now see that you were right and I was wrong. There's just no way to deal with these people. I'm really sorry I got you into this mess, but I'm going to get you out of it, I promise."

Mandelbaum looked at him steadily for a minute without saying a word.

"No, it's not your fault. It's the fault of your God for making Hitler ... or for making me a Jew," he said with a forced smile. "But, seriously, do you really think I need any more of your kind of help? I've got it all figured out, what I'm going to do. I'm not going to wait for them. I refuse to be a passive victim. They'll have to take me kicking and screaming. Maybe I can even get a few of them before they get me. But that's if they catch me by surprise. What I really want to do, if I can get away in time, is to go into the woods like the m*etsavennad*. Hitler and Stalin will have their day, but they won't last forever. I can wait them out. We Jews are good at that."

Bold words, Kingsepp thought, but does he know where to find a safe hiding place? Maybe he'll at least let me help him with that. "You know that I spent a month in a bunker up near Soovere. It's intact and still a good hiding place, almost impossible to find. No one is using it now, so it would be perfect for you. I know a trustworthy young man who can take you there and keep you supplied with food and things. He'll also keep an eye out for German patrols and warn you if necessary. I strongly suggest you go there tonight – before it's too late."

The next morning, when Kingsepp passed by the shop, it was locked up. He could see that nothing inside had changed, but he knew that Mandelbaum was gone. That was confirmed later in the day when Juhan dropped by the manse. "The pigeon's in the coop," he said enigmatically. Kingsepp caught himself beginning to smile. "It's not a joke," he said. "I'm counting on you to keep him safe, so don't tell anyone else. Let's keep this a secret, just between you and me."

Chapter Twenty-Three

Three days later, Kingsepp was awakened by the sound of a car arriving in the front yard of the manse. His wife, who had jumped out of bed, was peering out the window. She was in a tizzy. "Get dressed, Karla," she shouted at him. "You can still get out the back door. I'll try to delay them."

"Calm down, Evely. I'm not going anywhere. Do you really think I can outrun a car?" As he spoke, he too peered out the window while pulling on his trousers.

"It's Major Hauptmann, from Paide," he said. "I'm going down to talk to him. I don't think they're here for any trouble, not the way they are dressed." In his mind, however, he wasn't entirely convinced of that. Could it be that they had found Mandelbaum?

The major, wearing his full-dress uniform, was just as smiling and gracious as he had been when Kingsepp had visited him in Paide.

"Sorry to wake you, Pastor, but we have a little problem. Seems like one of our officers accidentally shot himself last night. For various reasons, which I don't want to go into, we need to bury him right away. Will you please help us with the funeral?"

Kingsepp, who had not been aware he had been holding his breath, exhaled deeply. "Of course I will, *Herr Sturmbannführer*."

"I've already had the grave dug in your cemetery, Hauptmann continued, "so if you can get what you need, I'll bring you there right away."

"Do you mind me asking, *Herr Sturmbannführer*, what is the name of this unfortunate man?"

"Not at all. He's actually someone I believe you know quite well, Lieutenant Klapp from the detachment here. The poor fellow was cleaning his pistol and must have overlooked a bullet in the chamber."

Kingsepp's heart sank. That was no accident, he thought. He had seen the anguish on Klapp's face. Quite obviously he had felt beyond redemption and had chosen to end his pain. He should have known that Klapp needed more than a prayer to sustain him, and felt a surge of guilt for not having stayed with him through his dark night. But of course, there were two people who needed his help and he had had to choose between them. He had done so, hoping that Klapp would be a survivor. How could he have predicted suicide? Or was it that? Kingsepp remembered the trace of a smile on Hauptmann's face when he had mentioned Klapp's name.

At the cemetery, three men were standing beside an open grave at the far end where trees partly hid them from sight. A closed coffin was already in the hole. His sexton stood at the ready with his shovel beside the mound of dirt he had excavated. Beside him, Kingsepp was startled to see, stood Karl Kivisik, dressed rather nattily in civilian clothes and smiling at him. Hauptmann, who had seen the shock of recognition on the pastor's face, also smiled. "I believe you've met my interpreter," he said. "You and I, of course, don't need him, but I thought he would help in dealing with your sexton. If you don't mind, Pastor, let's get on with it. I want to get back to Paide in time for breakfast."

It was a simple funeral, less than Klapp deserved, the pastor thought. No homily and no eulogies, no singing of hymns; just the reading of the order of service for burial and a short prayer he had added, beseeching the Lord to welcome his long-suffering child, Werner Klapp, to eternal life by His side.

Hauptmann and his adjutant drove off immediately, as though they did not want to be seen by the villagers. Before he left, however, Hauptmann told the pastor that "his interpreter" would be staying behind for a short while to discuss some matters with the pastor, if that was acceptable. "You may also wish to reminisce about the past," the major added with a smile.

"Well Pastor, long time no see," Kivisik said after the major's departure. "I suspect I may still be *persona non grata* around here, so why don't we go back to your rectory, where it's more private. I hear things are back to normal, so maybe you could offer me a proper breakfast before we talk."

142

The man hasn't changed at all, Kingsepp thought. *Still as brazen as ever. And how on earth did he get to be one of Hauptmann's men? Birds of a feather, I guess.*

The farm-style breakfast of sausages and bacon, fried eggs, boiled potatoes, and dark rye bread slathered with butter that Mrs. Sillaots brought in was exactly to Kivisik's taste, and he kept piling more onto his plate.

"Hauptmann eats well," he said, when he noticed the pastor staring at him, "but he's too busy smiling to eat much. I never seem to get enough when he's around."

After another helping, he poured himself some more tea and lit a cigarette. "So Karl, I guess you're surprised to see me alive? Frankly, so am I. For a while there, I didn't think I'd make it. But I knew I could trust you. You're probably the last honest man in Estonia. So thank you. I bet you're also wondering what Hauptmann wants with you? It's a good question. And I have the answer."

Kingsepp remained quiet. He was curious but didn't want to drag this out more than necessary. Let him get on with it, he thought.

"You, Karl, are a sly dog," Kivisik began. "All that time you were pretending to me that you didn't know the man who was murdered. Pretending is the right word, isn't it? You did know him, and that he was looking for a sword that belonged to Count von Mentzenkampf. But I bet you didn't know that Major Hauptmann is a cousin of the Mentzenkampfs, and that he has promised his cousin that he will recover that sword."

"Not that again!" the pastor broke in angrily. "This is total nonsense you're spouting. I never knew that man and I don't know anything about the missing sword."

"Have it your way," Kivisik said. "But you're going to have to tell that to Hauptmann. He wants to find that sword, and he's convinced you know where it is. I guarantee you that it would be better for you if you told me, before he talks to you himself." He paused for a moment. "You seem to have a knack for getting on the wrong side of authority, Karl. Hauptmann already believes you are a subversive type, a Jew lover and a corrupter of his soldiers. He thinks young Klapp would still be alive except for you. If I were you, I'd think twice before I upset him any more."

"I'm shocked by what you are telling me," Kingsepp said. "I haven't done anything to corrupt anyone. I am just a pastor trying to do my duty. I can understand why Zhukov may have thought I was subversive, because your former masters wanted to eradicate all religion. But the Germans believe in God; Luther was a German. A lot of Germans are Lutherans. Why should Hauptmann hate me?"

"If you don't understand," Kivisik said, "I can't explain it to you. Just trust me. He does not like your type, and he would have no qualms about killing you, as he has had done to so many others. You did me a favor. I will do one for you. I strongly urge you to tell me where the sword is. It could save your life."

"Look here, Kivisik," the pastor said, almost shouting. "I would tell you if I could. I don't care about any damned sword. I don't have it and I don't know where it is. Anyway, what makes you think I do?" he added more calmly.

"All I can tell you is what he told me," Kivisik answered. "Like I said, Hauptmann is the cousin of Count von Mentzenkampf. You know who he is, right? Well, the Count's family had in its possession the sword that Lembit is supposed to have used at a battle in 1217 where he was killed...."

"I know all that history," the pastor interjected. "What I don't know is why anyone would think I am involved in anything to do with that sword."

"That's simple enough. You thought you were clever in concealing your ownership of the Metsa Talu farm. You may have fooled us, but Hauptmann knows that the Evely Lepik who is listed as the inheritor of Jüri Reimann's farm is your wife. So why all that subterfuge... unless you had something to hide, eh? So what could that thing be that you're hiding? Jüri's father found the sword, and Hauptmann thinks the person who stole it back had to be Jüri. But he's dead, so Hauptmann is convinced that you are hiding the sword, hoping to use it as a symbol to stir up a mass uprising of Estonians against the Germans ... or against the Russians, if that's the way the cards fall."

The pastor couldn't help but snort. How ridiculous could anyone be!

"Why are you laughing? Hauptmann is deadly serious. His agents have discovered a diary written by Toomas Sillaots...."

The pastor gave an involuntary groan.

"Ah, so you recognize that name? Of course you do. You know him as the leader of a patriotic guerrilla force that fought against the Reds. To make a long story short, your name comes up several times in his diary as the possible guardian of the sword. He also mentions that he is trying to cultivate you so that you two could lead an uprising together. You can see why Hauptmann is taking this very seriously."

"He doesn't want to arrest you just yet, mainly because you're a pastor. But if you refuse to cooperate, I assure you that he will. I know his type. He sent me here because he thinks you and I are friends, which by the way, is another strike against you. He doesn't really like me either, and he doesn't trust me. He just uses people and then discards them. I owe you a favor, so I will help you if I can, but I'm afraid there isn't much I can do. These guys are worse than Zhukov, I assure you. My advice is to cooperate and hope he is in a good mood."

Kivisik paused to let his words sink in. "So what do you want me to tell Hauptmann? I have to tell him something when I get back." Kivisik fixed the pastor with an expectant stare, but Kingsepp was still thinking it over. How could he convince Hauptmann that he really had nothing to do with Sillaots's cockeyed plans and that he had never even heard of the sword until a few months ago and that he was being railroaded by an extraordinary series of coincidences. Truth had to be the way out of this morass. He would simply tell the truth.

"You can tell him that my connection to this sword is purely coincidental. I know nothing more about it than Hauptmann does. My wife's relationship to Jüri Reimann is the only reason Sillaots believed that I might know about the sword. I never met the man who was murdered, but apparently he believed in the same coincidence and was following me to find the sword. Sillaots caught on to him and killed the man after brutally torturing him to find out what he knew. Do you really think I would have anything to do with that kind of thing? I only know about it because Sillaots confessed his guilt in a letter he wrote that was given to me after his death. He also urged me to find the sword so that it could be used to rally Estonians. That part of his diary is true.

"But I never ever encouraged him or gave him any reason to think I shared his values. He was a romantic nationalist, one of those Taara believers who think they are the only true patriots. As you know, I have no time for anything like that. I even had a run-in with him when he started bringing his scouts to the rifle range during church hours. But you couldn't reason with him. I never spoke to him again until we had to share a bunker while I was hiding from your comrades. He was a brave soldier, but I felt that his judgment and sense of reality were impaired by his patriotic delusions. We are very different types of people. I would never consider joining up with him in anything."

Kingsepp paused briefly to catch his breath. "That's the truth, and if Hauptmann is as clever as he thinks he is, he will know that. I really can't add anything more."

Kivisik shrugged his shoulders. "Well, Pastor, I believe you. For both our sakes, I hope Hauptmann does also.... but I'm not sure that he will."

Chapter Twenty-Four

After his conversation with Kivisik, the pastor expected a quick summons to Paide by Major Hauptmann, but no call came. Another development, however, worried the pastor greatly. Werner Klapp, the tormented young German lieutenant, was replaced by someone more in the mold of Major Hauptmann. The day after arriving in Vändra, the dapper young officer, Lieutenant Otto Drexler, called on him at the rectory and wasted little time in nailing his colors to the mast.

"I've been informed that you are not exactly a friend of the *Reich*, Pastor. Be that as it may, I want to tell you that I will not tolerate any *anti-Reich* activities. You are a pastor and if you wish to remain a pastor, I will expect you to behave correctly in every way. I have my orders and I will carry them out. So be advised."

"If I may say something," the pastor said, "I have no intention of breaking any laws, but if God's laws are...."

Before he could continue, Drexler angrily broke in, "I am not here to negotiate. There is nothing to discuss; I have already told you how I intend to proceed. That is all I have to say. Good day, Pastor."

As usual, Mr. Männik had been right, the pastor thought. The Germans were no better than the Russians. They could do whatever they wanted, since their power was not held in check by any humanitarian scruples. They were anything but liberators.

Later that week, Mr. Männik dropped by the manse one afternoon, looking uncharacteristically distraught. "It's my son Andres," he said. "He wants to join that new Estonian Legion the Germans are setting up. It's not that he likes the Germans, but because he wants them to beat the Russians, or else the Reds will be back here to finish what they started three years ago. I've tried, but I can't seem to find the words to change his mind."

147

"I don't know if I can help you," the pastor said. "I've run into the same problem with my wife's younger brother, Mati. He's also planning to enlist, for the same reasons. He told her it's better to do that now. Then if the Germans win, they'll remember that the Estonians helped them and treat us better."

"Andres said that, too," Mr. Männik said, "but I think the young men are just frustrated doing nothing and want to feel that they can play a role somehow. What should happen is that the Russians and the Germans fight it out among themselves and leave us out of it."

"I can't imagine that ever happening," the pastor said. "The reason they are fighting, of course, is to see which of them can take over all of Europe, so it really doesn't matter which side wins. They're two sides of the same coin; there's no good in either of them. Have you heard what's going on in those new prison camps they've built in Lagedi, Vaivara and Klooga? I heard that they've been bringing in trainloads of Jews and Gypsies and homosexuals – and they're not just keeping them in prison; I heard they are killing them."

"Yes, I have heard that, too," Mr. Männik said. "It's so crazy I didn't believe it at first, but then I heard it from someone I trust one hundred percent. What's hardest to believe though is that this man told me some Estonians are mixed up in that business. Mostly as guards, he said, but that doesn't make them any less guilty. Who would believe our boys are capable of that? I'm sorry to say it, Pastor, but sometimes I wonder where God is in all this."

"I've felt that way myself and I can't just brush it off by saying that God works in mysterious ways," the pastor said wryly. "Sometimes I'm not sure what I believe any more. It's all very confusing. Look at my two brothers-in-law: Mati's older brother Mark was in the Estonian Army, which has been taken over by the Red Army, so now he is off somewhere in Russia fighting against the German Army, which his little brother is planning to join. It doesn't make any sense."

The two men sat silently for a moment.

"You know, of course," the pastor said, "if what we heard about the prison camps is true, then that's the kind of thing your son or my brother-in-law could end up doing if they don't get sent to the front. My sense of it is that the Germans don't really trust us very much; we're not Teutons, after all. The only use they have for us is to do their dirty work. Unfortunately, they have found some takers among us, just like the Russians did. I think the lads who have fled to Finland to carry on the fight against Russia there are doing the only right thing. I think that's what we should encourage our boys to do if they insist on fighting."

That evening, as the Kingsepps and Tädi sat over their supper, the pastor mentioned that Mr. Männik had dropped by the rectory earlier with the same kind of concerns that Evely had been expressing. "His son wants to join the Estonian Legion. He hasn't been able to dissuade him either."

"Just like Mati," his wife said. "I even asked him what he would do if he had to face his brother Mark in battle, and he just dismissed the idea. 'That won't happen,' he said. 'But it could easily be some other Estonians,' I told him, and he said he'd have to deal with that if it ever occurred. I told him it would be too late by then. What am I going to do Karla? He's barely nineteen. I have to stop him."

"Have your parents tried to talk to him?" Kingsepp asked.

"You know he doesn't care what Isa says. Ema has tried several times, but it's no use; he just refuses to listen. She suggested he go to Finland and join the army there if he was dead set on fighting..."

"That's what I was going to suggest," the pastor broke in. "Both Mr. Männik and I think that's the only real alternative."

"Well, it's not an alternative any more," Evely said. "Mati did actually look into it, but it's too late. The Germans have closed the ports. There's no way to get across to Finland any more. He says he can't just sit around here doing nothing while the Russians might be winning."

Chapter Twenty-Five

While the news from the war front remained everyone's major pre-occupation, the pastor also had to deal with a sudden spate of local issues. Some days, like this one, were particularly wearisome, Kingsepp thought one Monday as he lit his fourth cigarette of the morning. He had tried to resist, but sometimes, when he desperately needed to take his mind off the matters at hand, he became a chain smoker. Luckily he wasn't a drinking man, or it could have been four shots of vodka, he mused.

Olavi Kadarbik was the latest problem, actually a recurring one. No matter how hard he tried, the pastor could never make the cantankerous old farmer see reason. That morning was the third time since his arrival in Vändra that Olavi had come to complain that the pastor had singled him out in his sermon as an example of bad behavior.

On the first occasion, nearly four years ago, the pastor had preached a sermon on marriage. Although holy matrimony was not a sacrament *per se*, the pastor had said, Martin Luther himself had stated clearly that there was no higher condition in the eyes of God than the estate of marriage. Cohabiting without marriage, the pastor said, was sinful, and was to be avoided by Christians. He had gone on to say that women, especially, also needed to be aware of the financial and social hazards of cohabitation. He then offered the example of an unnamed woman in a cohabiting couple who had been abandoned by her partner when she became seriously ill. There are no safeguards for women in such relationships, the pastor had warned.

After that service Olavi had stormed into the rectory demanding to know why the pastor had chosen to expose his dirty laundry and mock him in front of the whole congregation. He and his partner had passed themselves off as a married couple, so how did the pastor even know their circumstances, especially since their relationship had ended before the pastor had arrived in Vändra?

The pastor had tried to explain that while his example was drawn from real life, it had been taken from a parish situated more than 100 kilometers from Vändra, and therefore could not have referred to Olavi. He then kept quiet to let those facts sink in and indeed it seemed to him that Olavi had been mollified, when the prickly farmer suddenly blurted out "Yes, that may be so, but how much did Paul Tõllason pay you to use that particular example?" It was clear to the pastor that he was dealing with a closed mind and that Olavi would continue to believe what he wanted to believe, especially when it concerned his neighbor Tõllason, with whom he had long had a running feud.

Now years later, Olavi had arrived that morning bristling about yet another example of the pastor singling him out for mockery. The sermon the previous day had been about forgiving trespasses, and the pastor had mined yet another example from his boyhood memories. His father's neighbor, who had an adjoining hayfield, he said, had once mowed several large swaths of hay from his father's field, which he had gathered and taken away. When his father pointed this out to his neighbor, the man had vehemently denied his trespass. Instead of shouting back, his father had taken the trouble to invite the neighbor to the field where he pointed out the boundary marker posts, which to be honest, had fallen down. The neighbor thereupon admitted his mistake and a potentially debilitating feud of the kind so vividly described by Anton Tammsaare in his classic novel of rural life, Tõde ja Õigus, ("Truth and Justice") had been averted.

His father and his neighbor had done the right thing, the pastor had said, by accepting what Christ taught us about forgiving trespasses. "Not only is that how we can gain the Kingdom of Heaven, but it also allows us to live in peace and harmony in this world."

"That was very clever of you, Pastor," Olavi had told him, "using your father to camouflage your real intention. But you didn't fool me. I know that pig of a neighbor of mine put you up to it again. How much is Tõllason paying you? I can pay you more. Look!" As he spoke, Olavi pulled a greasy wallet from his jacket pocket and started throwing ten-*kroon* notes on the pastor's desk. "Take as many as you want. Take them all; I've got plenty more. Just tell some stories about Tõllason next week. That's what you would do if you were an honest man."

The pastor stared stonily at Olavi, without saying a word or making any movement. Olavi stared back, but after a minute or so, he picked up the banknotes and turned on his heel and walked out. "So that's how it is," he tossed over his shoulder as he left.

After the outer door had closed with an audible bang, Miss Soosaar knocked lightly and entered the pastor's inner office, looking apprehensive. "Are you all right, Pastor? I was going to fetch Hannes or Jukku if he stayed any longer. You know that he used to do this kind of thing to the old pastor, too. So it's not anything to do with you. He's just a silly old man."

"Thanks, Hilda," the pastor said. "I know I haven't done anything to annoy him, but sometimes I can't help but think there should be something more I can do to help a person like him. Maybe I'll talk to the doctor tomorrow... Hmm... I thought I heard voices out there. Is there someone else waiting to see me?"

"I'm afraid so, but she looked a little faint, so I suggested she step out for some air. Anyway, I'm sure you can use a moment or two for yourself. I'll bring her in as soon as you're ready."

Hilda's a real jewel, the pastor thought. Always thinking of the other person. Too much even, for her own good. Judging by the little bit he had overheard through the closed door, it looked as if she was again being a mother hen to someone. He had sensed for some time now that she was particularly solicitous and helpful to the young women in the parish, especially those who had been wounded by love. The pastor had once asked her why that was so and she had hesitantly confided in him her own story of broken dreams.

Hilda had been engaged at the age of 19 to the younger son of a well-to-do farmer in the parish. But the young man had been conscripted into the Tsar's army to fight in the Russo-Japanese War and had been reported killed in far-off Manchuria in 1904. She had loved him and had looked forward to his return so they could be married, so much so that for years she had refused to believe he was dead. No one had ever found his body and since there was no grave, she had kept alive the faint hope that there had been a mistake and that he would return.

After several years had passed, another young man, from a neighboring farm, had courted her but she had gently brushed him off. She had continued to live with her parents and had made the church the center of her life, taking over the secretary's job thirty years ago, all the while looking after her aged mother, who was nearly 90 now. The spurned suitor had reconciled himself to the situation and had become her best friend, though never a lover. He would drive Hilda and her mother to church every Sunday and to the manse on the days that she staffed the rectory office. To see them together, so loving and pleasant to each other, like an old married couple, one would never guess that beneath those sunny exteriors had once run deep currents of unrequited passion.

After five minutes had gone by, there was a gentle tap on the door and Hilda entered the office with an anxious-looking young woman in tow. "This is Elva Jürisson," Hilda said. "I believe she needs your help, Pastor, so I'll leave you two to sort things out."

Turning to the young woman, she said, "Remember what I told you, Elva. If anyone can help you, it's the Pastor. So tell him everything you told me. Don't hold anything back."

The pastor, who could see that Elva was extremely nervous, stopped Miss Soosaar before she could leave. "Could we have some tea please, Hilda? I'm quite thirsty and I'm sure that Elva might like some too. And if there are any left, could you also bring us a few of those biscuits Tädi baked the other day."

While they waited for the tea the pastor passed the time by recalling out loud that Elva had been among the students in his first confirmation class nearly seven years ago. "Everything was new to me then and I don't remember all of you very clearly, but I believe you were one of the bright ones in the class. I remember your parents were very proud of you."

By the time Miss Soosaar came back with the tea, he could see that Elva was losing some of the deer-in-the-headlights expression with which she had entered the room. She had even allowed a slight smile to play on her face when the pastor mentioned her Confirmation class, but he noticed that her hand still trembled when she tried to raise her tea cup. He quickly glanced away while she used her other hand to steady the cup on her second attempt.

"Nothing like a good cup of tea," the pastor said when she put down the cup. "So what might be the trouble? Something we can fix quite quickly, I hope."

Elva tried to speak but broke down before she could get out more than a word or two. "I want to get married," she finally managed to say between sobs.

"Well, that's not anything to cry about," the pastor said. "Unless there's more to the story than that," he added, which in fact turned out to be the case.

She was pregnant, Elva said, and her strait-laced father had not taken it well. She had brought disgrace on the family, he had told her. As far as he was concerned, she was no longer his daughter. She would have to leave his house and hope that her lover would look after her.

"I think we can deal with that," the pastor broke in. "I know what your father is like. But I also know that he loves you, and I'm sure that once you're married your father will reconsider and all will be well. It's not the first time something like this has happened, you know. I'll speak to your father."

"I don't think he will change his mind. In any case, it won't help," Elva broke in sobbing. "You see, my...uh, friend ... is a German and he's under arrest now, and they won't let me see him."

This was a complication the pastor had not expected. He started to reach for his cigarettes but caught himself in time. "Yes, that could be tricky, if the Germans are involved. But let's not give up hope," the pastor said. "How did you end up in this predicament? You better start from the beginning and tell me the whole story."

Elva tried hard to tell a coherent story, but she was nervous and he had to prompt her several times when she left out important information or wandered off into inconsequential details. As best he could make out, the story was that Elva had been brought up very strictly. She was a pretty girl and several boys had been attracted to her, but none of them was good enough for her father, who shooed them all away. After a while, no boys bothered to call on her, especially after a few of the disappointed suitors had demonstrated their displeasure by hauling her father's farm wagon up on his barn roof one night. "You see what young men are like," he had told her and redoubled his protective efforts.

155

But last fall, during *Oktooberfest,* Elva had convinced her parents to set up a booth where she could sell the mittens, scarves and hats she and her younger sisters had knitted all winter. People had liked their wares, especially a German soldier who came by several times, each time buying something that Elva had made. He was very pleasant, she said, and unlike her parents, talked to her intelligently. It was clear to her that he liked her, and she found herself warming up to him a little more each time he came by. When he proposed to visit her on his day off duty, she agreed to sneak out of the house to meet him.

One thing led to another and they soon fell deeply in love. When she discovered she was pregnant, instead of casting her off, he had insisted they would get married. If his superior officer refused to allow that, he said he would run off with her. As it turned out, that's exactly what happened. His request was turned down and in desperation he had snuck out of his barracks to go to her.

But he had been caught quickly and now was in jail. When she heard what had happened, she couldn't control her emotions and spent two full days weeping before her parents wormed the story out of her. Instead of the empathy she had hoped for, she got only rejection.

"I don't know what to do or where to go," Elva said, sobbing. "I can't go home any more, and I can't tell anyone else about this. That would only make things worse."

"There's no problem about a place to stay," the pastor said. "We have plenty of room here, and you can stay as long as it takes to set things right. My wife will look after you. I can't promise that the rest of your troubles can be fixed that easily, but I will try.

"Let's get you settled in, and then I'll go see your father and Lieutenant Drexler to see how we can get you married. What's your young man's name, by the way?"

"Joachim, Joachim Hertzmann," she whispered. "Thank you, Pastor."

An hour later, the pastor was knocking on the door of the Jürisson farmhouse. This wasn't going to be an easy discussion, he knew, having had encounters with August Jürisson previously. August was high church from the old school, a man who believed in literal interpretations of the Bible and would think nothing of correcting the pastor if he believed the pastor had taken liberties with a Biblical text. He was also a staunch patriot, who no doubt was doubly offended by his daughter's choice of a German lover.

As he had expected, August was unyielding. Premarital sex was nothing more than fornication, he said, and that was an unforgivable sin.

"I'm not sure there are any unforgivable sins," the pastor began, but was quickly interrupted.

"I would expect better of you, Pastor. Surely you are familiar with Matthew 5, verses 29 and 30." August picked up the Bible on the table beside him and read out loud the passage that he had obviously been contemplating:

"If your right eye makes you stumble, tear it out, and throw it from you; for it is better for you that one of the parts of your body perish, than for your whole body to be thrown into hell."

"Jesus said that, you know, and it's very clear," August continued. We have no choice but to cast off anyone, even our own child, who is an abomination in the eyes of the Lord."

The pastor had been prepared for this. "But if you read a little further, in verse 44," he replied, "you will see that Jesus wants us to practise forgiveness, even of our enemies. And in Matthew, Chapter 6, verses 14 and 15, he tells us explicitly:

"For if you forgive men for their transgressions, your heavenly Father will also forgive you. But if you do not forgive men, then your Father will not forgive your transgressions."

"Listen to me, August. I urge you not to take your values from what is after all an ambiguous passage in the Bible, but to follow what Christ teaches us in The Lord's Prayer and the Golden Rule – to do unto others as we would want them to do unto us."

August was actually paying attention, the pastor could see. It seemed clear that he was torn between his religious scruples and his love for his daughter, and wanted desperately to find an honest way out of his predicament. The pastor, whose views on sin and human weakness had evolved over the years, re-emphasized the need for forgiveness.

"We have to listen to Christ when He admonishes us in Matthew Chapter Seven that we should not judge others, lest we be judged ourselves. I urge you to accept the words of our Lord and have mercy on your child. Christ says: '*Ask, and it shall be given to you; seek and you shall find. Knock and it shall be opened to you.*' Well, your daughter is knocking at the door of your heart, and Christ is urging you to open that door. Are you able to listen to Him?"

August hung down his head and sighed. "I do hear Christ's message, Pastor, and I hate the sin, not the sinner. But the sinner must repent and must put aside the sin and return to the path of righteousness. If my daughter is able to do that, I will take her back into the family, even though I have two other daughters for whom I fear this could be a bad example."

Having secured August's somewhat grudging agreement, the pastor hurried over to the village in the hope of getting to see *Oberleutnant* Drexler.

Not only was Drexler in, but he agreed to see the pastor immediately.

"I was planning to pay you a visit anyway," he told the pastor. "It seems like we have a problem."

"I hope it's a little one," the pastor replied. "I have been to see the father of the girl and he is agreeable to a marriage. If you feel the same way, then there will be no problem."

"Oh, is that so? I don't think it is as easy to fix as that," the lieutenant answered. "You see, the *Führer* does not approve of the mongrelisation of races, particularly the German race. I'm afraid a marriage is out of the question."

The pastor's face fell. This was beyond anything he had expected.

"And there are other complications," Drexler said, almost snickering at the pastor's bewilderment. "You see, young Joachim is in the stockade. He was arrested after going AWOL to see this floozy of his and was convicted by a court-martial. This is wartime, so desertion is a capital offense. I recommended that he face the firing squad."

The pastor gasped. "You can't be serious. He just went to visit his girlfriend because she is pregnant. And she is not a floozy. She is a decent girl who happened to fall in love."

"The law is the law, Pastor. Surely you understand that. Without the law, everything falls apart. That's what makes us different from you and the Russians, why we will always win. Because we are a law-abiding people. People who break the law get a trial, and if they are convicted they have to be punished as an example to other would-be criminals. Joachim broke the law. He has been tried by a court-martial and has been found guilty. So now he must pay for his crime.

"I can't believe what I am hearing," the pastor said. "I will speak to Major Hauptmann."

The lieutenant smiled. "Go ahead. The Major is well acquainted with this case and agrees with me that the punishment must be exemplary. As it happens, however, he has a different idea about what the punishment should be. Since it is a time of war, and the army always needs men at the front, the Major has commuted his death sentence and is sending Joachim to the south to join the Sixth Army fighting in Stalingrad."

"He is leaving" – he glanced at his watch – "in 15 minutes, so as you can see there will be no possibility of a wedding, even if we permitted it, which, of course, we do not. So good day, Pastor. And I suggest you try harder to teach your girls not to be floozies."

It was with a heavy heart that the pastor communicated this information to Elva and her parents later that day. Elva, as he had expected, was beyond consolation, but her parents seemed relieved that Joachim was out of the picture. They said they would contact Mrs. Jürisson's sister in Tartu, where their daughter would be able to have her baby far from the prying eyes of their neighbors. She was young and would recover, they said. Maybe she would even find some nice Estonian man there who wouldn't mind marrying a "war widow" with a child.

It wasn't what he had hoped for, but the pastor accepted it as the best that could be done. Going to bed that night, he said a special prayer for both Elva and her Joachim. With God's help, maybe they could still find a way to be reunited.

Chapter Twenty-Six

As in the previous year, early snowstorms were the harbingers of a severe winter. Two blizzards in late November piled up huge drifts that blocked the roads for weeks and kept most adults housebound nearly until Christmas. For the children, however, it was like an early start to the holidays since the schools were closed and there was plenty of snow for sledding and building forts and snowmen. Then quite dramatically, the sun broke though the clouds and weather conditions eased off just in time for Christmas. That surely was a sign from on high that their lives were changing for the better, many villagers were quick to assert. The pastor, however, resisted such predictions; the war was as deadly as ever, and nothing he was aware of warranted optimism. For himself, he was just glad that he would be able to go out again and get some exercise to counteract the enforced idleness of the past weeks, as well as the accumulated effects of rich holiday foods. He particularly looked forward to the re-opening of the secondary school where he was once again teaching two classes of Religious Studies each week. He had missed the mental stimulation that interacting with students provided, as well as the invigorating walks into the village.

On his first day back, he left the manse earlier than necessary, thinking that he would take a look at Mandelbaum's shop. He had heard that there had been a fire there a couple of nights ago, and he wanted to see what was left of it. The familiar route took him past the three-storey house recently taken over by the SS officers who were now playing a larger role in the administration of the village. He hadn't expected to see Major Hauptmann's staff car parked in front of the house, and he seriously considered turning back. That would be cowardly, he finally decided, and so he pressed ahead. He had passed the car and was starting to breathe more easily when he heard the major's voice.

"How nice to see you, Pastor Kingsepp. Going to buy cigarettes, I presume," the major added with a knowing smile. "Well, I can save you the trouble. There's plenty of smoke at his place, but the old Jew doesn't live there anymore. Perhaps you knew that already?"

The pastor said nothing, but turned to acknowledge the major.

"I'm glad we bumped into each other," the major continued. "I wanted to congratulate you on what a fine young man your brother-in-law is. I had almost given up on you and your family, but I can see that would have been a mistake. I hope the other young men around here will follow his example.

"Oh, by the way," he said, still smiling, "I don't think you'll see anything interesting in the old Jew's shop. My men, who put out the fire, did find a sword in the ashes, but, unfortunately, it wasn't the one belonging to my cousin. However, I do believe what you told Kivisik. I don't think you're the kind of man who would get involved in the sort of things your friend Toomas Sillaots dreamed about. And speaking of former friends, you might be interested to hear that your namesake Kivisik is no longer with us. No, don't look so startled. He won't be needing your professional services. I've appointed him to supervise the Estonian guards at Vaivara. I think that's more in line with his talents." With a smile and a wave of his arm, he climbed into his car and was gone, leaving a shaken and perplexed pastor to hurry back to face his class.

Afterwards, reflecting on what the major had told him, the pastor felt relieved that at least Hauptmann seemed to believe he was not implicated in the saga of the sword. Still, there were a lot of unanswered questions that he was curious about. After lunch, when Evely had taken the baby off for his nap, he decided to again ask Tädi, who was clearing the table, about whether Jüri had left any papers or packages that no one had looked at yet.

"I'm still curious about that sword I mentioned to you once. I don't remember if I said at the time that it's supposed to be the sword of Lembit and that it was Jüri's father who had found it buried in Count von Mentzenkampf's garden. The man who told me about it thought that maybe Jüri had somehow got it back and hidden it away somewhere, maybe at Metsa Talu."

Tädi stopped in her tracks. "How could he do that? He never had the sword, as far as I know. Unless you're suggesting that he stole it and didn't tell me. But that's not the kind of man he was. I'm surprised you would even think that possible." She was positively glaring at him.

"Now, now, Tädi, don't get me wrong. You know I would never think Jüri would do anything criminal. But let me put everything on the table. I've been told there are men out there who would lie, cheat, steal and even kill to get their hands on that sword, assuming it still exists. They're probably wrong, but somehow they have got it into their heads that Jüri ended up with the sword. You – all of us, really – will not be completely safe as long as those men believe Jüri hid it."

"I don't like the sound of that, " Tädi said more quietly, "but what are we supposed to do? If you want me to, I'll swear on a stack of Bibles that Jüri never had anything to do with any sword. Evely thought we had a picture of the Count standing in front of a sword that may have been the one you are looking for, but we couldn't find it. Anyway, that was the only old sword in the manor house and as I told you before, I think the young Count took it back to Germany when he left."

"That's the problem Tädi, the Count never took it to Germany. Someone in his employ was supposed to bring it to a silversmith for repairs but seems to have walked off with it instead. At least, that's what the Count believes, and he has asked his cousin Major Hauptmann to get it back. For some reason the major thinks Jüri was that employee, and that he stashed the sword away somewhere," the pastor said, adding almost as an afterthought, "probably to keep it safe for the Count."

Tädi looked skeptical.

"Of course, if Jüri was that employee, another possibility is that someone stole the sword from him," the pastor said hurriedly.

"No, it can't be anything like that," Tädi said. "Jüri was already very sick when the Count left, and there was no way he could have gone out on errands of that kind. Anyway, we had no secrets between us. He would certainly have told me if he was involved, but he didn't, so he couldn't have been."

The conviction in her voice was so palpable the pastor couldn't doubt that she was telling the truth. How could he have thought that this kindly, patently transparent woman might have harbored dark secrets? He felt ashamed of his earlier suspicions.

"So that's it. Just like I thought, we're still at a dead end," he said. "I guess I can tell you now that for a while Major Hauptmann thought I was somehow involved in this, because of my connection to you and Jüri. But he seems to have accepted that that was just a coincidence. At least that's what he told me, though I'm not sure we can trust anything he says. Anyway, I don't know what else we can do about it, so let's just forget this ever happened."

"As far as I'm concerned," Tädi answered, "nothing ever did happen."

Picking up a pile of papers from the sideboard, the pastor said, "I still have some work to do, Tädi. Would you please tell Evely I've gone back to the rectory?"

He had barely sat down at his desk when Miss Soosaar tapped on the door. "There's an important message for you, Pastor. Your brother called to say your father fell off a ladder and broke his hip. Apparently he is all right and is being looked after in the Jõgeva Hospital, but he has been asking for you."

"Thank you, Hilda," the pastor said. "Did my brother say I should go there right away or would it be all right to wait until after the Sunday service?"

"He didn't say anything about that, but I gathered that it isn't an emergency," she said.

"That's a relief. I'll leave Sunday afternoon, then. If I go right after church, I can be there by evening. If everything is all right, I'll be back in three or four days. Even with the big snowdrifts on the road, I should be able to get through easily now that I have Tasuja back."

164

Chapter Twenty-Seven

On Saturday evening, the pastor was getting ready for bed when he remembered he had forgotten to check a quotation he intended to use in his sermon the next morning. "I'll be right back," he told Evely and headed off through the house to his office in the far wing.

He had barely switched on the light, when he heard a tapping at the frost-covered window. Peering in was a rather wild-looking man with unkempt hair and a bushy beard, all bundled up in a ragged, oversized winter coat. It wasn't anyone he recognized, so he approached the window cautiously for a closer look. The man was pointing at himself and mouthing a word slowly, repeating it several times before the pastor understood: "M...A...N...D...E...L...B...A...U...M."

"I didn't recognize you; you're so thin," the pastor said, opening the door and quickly ushering him in. "You must have lost about ten kilos. And you don't look too well."

"Oh, I'm all right, but thanks for asking. The food wasn't so hot at that hotel you found for me, especially when Juhan would skip his visits for a week or two. But I'm not complaining. I could always find a few worms or bugs, and moss is tasty."

"Ah, the inner you hasn't changed at all," the pastor said with a smile. "I'm sure Juhan did the best he could, though the weather has been awful and he may have had to lie low once in a while. But tell me, what are you doing here? You're taking a big risk. Someone is bound to see you."

Mandelbaum sighed. "I had to get out of there. It was too cold. But mostly I was going crazy. I kept asking myself, 'What am I doing here, hiding like a rabbit in a hole while the dogs are circling around?' So I made up my mind. There's no point to this. Even if the Germans lose, it could take years, and would I be any better off if the Russians win?"

"But," the pastor said, "you always told me you wouldn't allow them to take you. So what else can you do?"

"I thought about a lot of things while I was there. Even getting hold of a weapon and becoming a one-man guerrilla force. 'An eye for an eye and tooth for a tooth,' I thought. Get a few of them before they get me. But then I thought what would that accomplish? Nothing. I would be just like them. Finally I realized that what I really wanted was to see my children again... maybe for the last time. That's what would make me happy and then I wouldn't mind dying."

The pastor gave him a quizzical look. "How are you going to do that? The Nazis are on the lookout for people like you, and I'm sorry to say, some of my people would help them if they could."

"Oh, I know that. But I also knew that there was at least one person who would help me. You. If I can get away from this area where people might recognize me, I'd at least have a chance of getting to Latvia to look for my children. You can help me shave my beard and cut my hair. Then, after a bath and a change of clothes, I might be able to pass for a Christian. After all, the Nazis say they can tell a Jew by his smell."

"Oh Avraham, you don't know what's been going on. They're killing your people, anyone they can find. I'm afraid that even if you get to Riga, you won't find your children."

"I've thought of that, and I don't care. If they're dead, then it won't be so hard to join them," Mandelbaum said with a wry smile.

Just then Evely walked in. She looked uneasy after noticing Mandelbaum. "Oh I'm sorry. I didn't know you had a visitor, Karl. You said you'd be right back, so I got worried and came to see what you were doing."

"Evely," the pastor said, "I'd like you to meet Avraham Mandelbaum, an old friend. He is going to need our help to cut his hair and shave and take a bath. Then if you can find an old suit and maybe even a small cross on a neck chain, that would be good. And we should make up the bed in the spare room and maybe find some leftovers for him. But Evely, don't tell anyone about this. We have to do this ourselves. OK?"

As Evely went off to heat up some water and look for scissors and a razor, Avraham turned to the pastor. "You know, Karl, we have joked around a lot, but I want to tell you from my heart that you are a good man."

The pastor looked embarrassed. "I don't know about that. Believe it or not, I have sometimes done things that I'm ashamed of. When I was a boy we used to pick on Gypsies. If we had known any Jews, we probably would have harassed them too. We never saw what we had in common, only that they were different. That way, it wasn't so hard to be mean to them. I was young then, but I've always felt guilty about it ever since."

"You know, you should stop feeling guilty. I am sure your God has forgiven you long ago."

By the time Mandelbaum had been safely installed in the guest room and the pastor joined Evely in their bedroom, it was past midnight. "Karla, are you sure you're doing the right thing?" she immediately asked. "If anyone finds that J...jje...um, man here, we're going to be in serious trouble. I think you should send him on his way as soon as you can in the morning."

"You're right, practically speaking," Kingsepp answered, "but I don't think we have a choice. I always used to think that Jesus's saying that when you feed a beggar you are feeding me was a metaphor, but now I believe he meant it literally. If we want to call ourselves Christians that's what we have to do."

"I do agree with you Karla, but think of the children..."

"I have a plan, Evely, and if we're both careful, it should work out. I have to be at church in the morning, but I will say that you're not feeling well, so you can stay at home and make sure no one goes near the guest room. As soon as I get back, I'll eat a sandwich and drive off in the sleigh to visit my father as planned. The only difference is that Avraham will go with me, and as soon as we're out of this district he'll get off and make his own way to Riga."

"What if someone sees him with you? It's too dangerous..."

"I admit there is a bit of a risk, but I'll take the back roads. People are used to seeing me all over the parish, and he'll be well wrapped up. No one will give him a close look if he's with me, and if they do, they won't recognize him the way he looks now. It's the only chance he has. He'd never get out of here otherwise."

The next morning, after church, everything went as the pastor had predicted. About five kilometers down the road they passed a checkpoint but were quickly waved through by the young German soldier who was too busy stamping his feet against the cold to linger outside the guard hut. They had taken a southerly direction, both to avoid Paide and to bring Mandelbaum a little closer to the Latvian border. Soon the pastor would have to swing northeast if he was to get to his father's bedside in Jõgeva. A kilometer or so before the turnoff, Mandelbaum asked the pastor to stop.

"Like you," he said, "I have a confession to make. I wasn't sure whether I should tell you this, but since we may never meet again, I decided I have to. I owe you that. It's a long story, but I'll try to be quick." The pastor looked at him quizzically, before nodding in assent.

Mandelbaum began: "Once when Juhan was bringing me food, he stayed for a while and we ended up talking about you. Among other things, he told me how brave you had been the day a strange man came to your church planning to shoot you. I knew exactly what Juhan was talking about, but I didn't say anything to him because I was too ashamed of my part in that event...."

"I don't understand. What do you mean by 'your part'? the pastor interrupted. "How could you have been involved?"

"That's what I want to tell you now," Mandelbaum said. "But I have to give you some background first." The pastor, who knew the older man could sometimes be longwinded, sighed and said, "But remember I have to get to Jõgeva before dark."

Mandelbaum grinned and resumed his tale. "Back around the time when the Communists were taking over," he said, "one of Count von Mentzenkampf's staff – it may have been his steward – tried to sell me an antique sword." The pastor groaned, but didn't say anything. "I already had a couple of old swords in the shop that I couldn't sell and he wanted much more than I thought it was worth, so I sent him on his way. If I had known then what I learned about the sword later, I would have gladly bought it from him." He reflected for a moment. "Or maybe not...."

"Anyway, the man in the church, if I can call him that, since I never did learn his name, came to my shop a little later, looking for a sword. I showed him the two I had, but they weren't what he wanted. The mistake I made then was to tell him that one of the Count's employees had offered to sell me another antique sword.

He didn't believe me when I said I hadn't bought it. He asked me if the seller was related to you and wanted to know if you might have it. He hit me and called me a dirty Jew and threatened to kill me if I didn't tell him where it was. I was desperate to get rid of him, so I finally told him you probably had it, because I had once seen you leaving the church one night with a long parcel. I told him I didn't actually see where you went, because I didn't follow you."

"Ah, that must have been the night I buried the antique candlesticks and chalice from the church to keep them safe from the Communists," the pastor said. "But what were you doing out so late at night?"

"I often went walking after dark because I didn't feel all that safe during the day. There were always a few people around who used to taunt me," Mandelbaum said. "God forgive me, Pastor, I didn't mean you any harm. I guess I figured that if he thought *you* had the sword, he'd give up looking for it and crawl back under a stone. Anyway, before the man left, he told me he would go to see you the next day and that I had better not be lying. There was a lot of money at stake, he said, and he would stop at nothing to get his hands on the sword.

"That worried me. I realized I had made a huge mistake and I knew I had to warn you about him. I waited until it was dark to go to the manse, so no one would see me, but there was no one there. Then I went to the church, where I found that the door to the sacristy was unlocked, so I pinned a note to your cassock where you would see it. Then I thought that maybe I should alert someone else in case you needed help. I left similar notes at two farms where I knew the people went to church."

"When I found out later that the man had been murdered, I couldn't risk telling anyone what I had done. I'm truly sorry I got you involved, and I'm glad it all worked out for you in the end. But I still don't know how the man was killed. Juhan said he didn't do it, and I'm sure it wasn't you, so it remains a mystery. And I guess no one knows where the sword is since the steward has disappeared without a trace."

The pastor was dumbfounded. "So you were the one who left the note!" he exclaimed. "So that's how it all began – what a coincidence! That sword has caused a lot of trouble for a lot of people, and no one even knows if it really is what they think it is. You know it was my wife's uncle's father who found the sword in the first place. Then all those people thought I had inherited the sword and was hiding it. So when you told that man I had it, that just confirmed what he already suspected. Then sadly, Toomas Sillaots – I think you know who he was – had similar suspicions. He was the one who actually killed that man after torturing him to reveal what he knew, which turned out to be not much. Then Major Hauptmann, a cousin of the Mentzenkampfs, also thought I had something to do with it. I can tell you, that sword has caused me more than a few anxious moments. Worst of all, it was responsible for a murder."

"That makes me feel even worse," Mandelbaum said. "I had no idea I had caused you so much trouble. I'm so sorry."

"Well, I guess that makes us even," the pastor said, "after all the trouble I caused you. And you shouldn't feel responsible for the murder; that fellow brought it on himself. I'm glad, though, that you told me this. It clears up something I have been wondering about for a long time. As far as I'm concerned, the sword can stay lost forever." He turned to embrace Mandelbaum. "I'd like to think we will meet again in better times, but somehow I don't think that will be possible. Goodbye, old friend. And may God bless you."

Mandelbaum clung to the embrace for several moments, before turning away to wipe his eyes. When he looked back he was smiling. "Goodbye Pastor, you're a proper *Mensch*."

Chapter Twenty-Eight

The Pastor arrived at the family farm quite late and rushed in expecting to see his father convalescing in his own bed. Instead, his mother clasped his hand and said, "Things are worse than we thought. Isa had some kind of stroke and is still in the hospital."

"I tried calling you," his brother broke in, "but Evely said you were already on your way. Take your coat off. Sit down and talk to Ema; I'll take care of your horse."

His mother had already put the kettle on while his brother was talking and was putting tea into the small china pot. "Bring the cups over from the shelf there," she instructed.

"What happened, Ema? I thought he just had a broken hip from falling off a ladder? What's all this about a stroke?"

"He broke his hip all right," his mother said. "He was clearing snow off the roof of the *saun* and lost his balance. At first they told us he would only have to stay in the hospital for a few days. He didn't seem to mind that and was in good spirits. He even told me he had been tired lately and could use a good rest. Then yesterday when I went to see him, he suddenly started talking nonsense and his face got all twisted and then he wasn't able to talk at all. The doctors say there's only a small chance he'll recover. Oh, Karla, he can't talk, and he can move only one arm...." She had to stop to wipe her eyes and blow her nose.

Karl went around the table to where she was sitting and put his arms around her. "It's hard, Ema. But whatever happens we have to accept God's will. We'll go to see Isa first thing in the morning. And I'll talk to the doctors. Maybe there's something they can do."

Karl, who wanted to see the doctor while he made his morning rounds, got up early to go to the hospital. Aleksander and his mother stayed behind to do the chores and were going to join him as soon as they could.

"We think he can still hear you," the doctor told him, "but it doesn't look like he will ever speak again. It was quite a massive stroke, and we don't have any way to deal with that except to make the patient as comfortable as we can. Another stroke is often fatal and that can happen any time. It's usually fairly quick."

Karl found it hard to look at his father in the hospital bed. Like many very sick parishioners that he had visited, his father looked gaunt and deathly pale, and almost lost in the bedding, nothing like the strong and active man he had been when he last saw him. He was very still. The only part of him that seemed alive were his eyes. They fixed on him and stayed there. They seemed inconsolably sad.

He had anticipated something like this and had brought all the necessities for giving his father Holy Communion. "Isa, I hope you can hear me. You are in God's hands now. We can't know what plans He has for anyone, but we have His promise of eternal life for those who accept His Son Jesus Christ as their Savior. By partaking of the sacred act of Communion, we are signifying that we believe in His infinite mercy and forgiveness and hope to sit with Him in glory forevermore."

Quietly saying the words of the sacrament, Karl placed a small piece of consecrated communion wafer in his father's mouth and allowed a small drop of wine from the chalice to touch his lips. As he moved on to the benediction, his father's eyes were still fixed on his face, but then suddenly their inner light was gone. Karl sat beside the bed for a moment, saying a prayer for his father's soul. Then he closed his father's eyes and crossed his hands on his breast. And waited for his mother.

It was a somber family that returned to the farmhouse. Karl knew from his experience of deathbeds at farmhouses that the widows rarely showed much emotion when their husbands died. So he wasn't surprised by his mother's silent stoicism. Death, whether of animals or people, was never far from farming families; they accepted it and moved on. Like so many other wives he had seen in these situations, she was very practical, and wanted to start organizing the funeral. She didn't want Karl to be inconvenienced, she said, by being kept away from his own family and parish any longer than necessary. Then she surprised him.

"Isa once told me, Karla, that he liked the idea that, when the time came, his son would bury him. He wasn't sure how you would feel about that, so he never asked you. He was worried that you might not feel up to it, I guess, but if you think you could do it, I know he would like that."

The request was unusual but not unprecedented. Karl knew of two or three similar cases, of which only one, in Keila, had been disastrous. The young pastor, who was burying his mother, broke down after barely starting the service. He tried several times to continue, but each effort was more painful than the previous one. Another pastor, a colleague who didn't really know the deceased but had come to support his friend, took over. He did his best, but without preparation and little knowledge of the deceased, his efforts were perfunctory and disappointing. Kingsepp didn't think that would happen to him; he told his mother that of course he would do as his father had wished. "I'm so happy to hear that," his mother said. "You're a good son."

Karl wasn't so sure of that. He knew that he had tried to be a good son, but it hadn't always been possible. Sometimes, especially when he was young, he had found his father overbearing and rigid and too quick with his belt. At those times, he had secretly hated his father. But as he grew older and saw more of life, he realized how hard it was to be a parent. On the whole, Isa had been a good father, he thought. He had certainly meant well and always acted according to his principles. It wasn't his fault that those principles were not always the ones Karl would have chosen to follow. His father had had only two winters of schooling and had had to learn most things on his own. "I couldn't possibly judge him harshly," Karl thought.

Aleksander, who had been out doing chores, caught Karl's eye as he came back in. "Do you want to come out for a smoke while Ema's fixing supper?" he asked. Karl nodded, put on his coat and followed his brother out. Walking silently side by side they made their way to the heated *saun*, a favorite sitting spot of their father, where they both lit up. "Karla, I don't quite know how to say this," Aleksander began, "but for a long time, I've been wanting Isa to die. Now that it has happened I feel guilty, and I'm miserable.

You're a pastor, so maybe if you can tell me I'm not a bad person, I'll be more able to cope with it."

"Of course you're not a bad person, Aleks...."

"No, no. I want you to listen to me before you say anything. You know I've always been supposed to inherit the farm. At first I was content enough to wait, but then I started thinking that it was never going to happen. I'd be an old man before Isa passed it on to me. I kept thinking of that and soon I started to wish that Isa would die. I didn't have anything against him; he was strict, but he always treated me fairly. I just wanted the farm so that I could get married and have a family. It didn't seem right that I couldn't do that, especially after you were already settled into your own family and job. And then he died. It's like it was my fault that he fell off the ladder and had a stroke. I feel guilty, and I feel that God is going to punish me."

Karl could see the misery on his brother's face. He wanted to put his arm around his shoulders, but his family had never hugged each other and he suspected his brother would only stiffen up, like his mother did when he had tried to do that. He considered his words carefully.

"I don't believe you should feel guilty," he began again. "It's quite common for people to think about things that would benefit them, but you certainly did not cause Isa's accident or his death. If we were to be judged only by our private thoughts, even the saints would be guilty. I certainly would be. I sometimes think about things I wouldn't want anyone else to know, but I also know that I would never do any of those things, so I put those thoughts aside and move on. What counts is what you do, and you have not done anything you need to be ashamed of. I think you should forget about those thoughts and stop worrying. You really have nothing to worry about; you're a good person."

The day of the funeral was one of the warmer clear days of the late winter, so there was a good turnout at the church and at the cemetery. He was glad for his mother's sake, even though she herself told him that some of the people were probably there as much to see him as they were to pay their respects to Isa. "I know these people," she said. "They came to see what kind of pastor you are." His mother didn't seem to mind that in the least, and was very pleased when some of them congratulated her on what a fine speaker her son was. "Your father would have liked that," she said as they sat at the end of the day, drinking tea in the kitchen. Before going to bed, Karl somewhat hesitantly told his mother he would leave the next morning. He had a parish to attend to and had been away from his family for a week and was missing them greatly. His mother pressed him to stay at least another day. "Do stay, Karla. I might never see you again."

"That's not true, Ema. I'll be back, I promise. Also, if you really feel that way, why don't you come to stay with us? We have plenty of room. And Evely's aunt is there, so you'll have company."

"This is my home, Karla. I'll never leave this place until they carry me out in a box to bury me beside your father," his mother replied. "Besides, you have your family and your wife's family. You don't need another old lady to quarrel with the other old lady. Also, Aleksander needs me much more than you do. All I pray for is that you can come back to bury me like you did your father."

"Of course I will Ema, but that won't be for many years yet. I'll be back to see you lots of times."

"I don't think so," his mother said. "Everyone is saying that the Germans are losing the war and the Russians will be back. Ida Tark told me after the funeral that she has heard that the Russians have sworn to close down all the churches and throw all the priests and pastors into prison when they get here. She said it's a shame, but you'd have to leave and I'd never see you again."

"Don't believe everything you hear, Ema. Maybe the United States of America will join the war and restore our freedom when they defeat the Nazis. Russia won't be able to do anything to us then." His mother only waved her hand, as if to say, 'you'll see I'm right.'

"I have to go, Ema. I promise I will be back to see you as often as I can." He gave her a hug and to his surprise, for the first time he could remember since he had been very little, she responded warmly, holding him tightly for a long time.

175

Chapter Twenty-Nine

Back in Vändra, Pastor Kingsepp learned from his wife that the rumor that the German drive to Moscow had faltered was true. "Mark has been missing since the battle at Velikiye Luki," she said. "Hilda doesn't know if he is dead or alive and is going crazy with worry. She says she could bear it if she knew definitely that he had died, but she has dreams in which he has been horribly mutilated, sometimes missing arms or legs, or has hideous wounds on his face. She's scared; she doesn't know how she will be able to look after her daughters by herself."

"That's so sad," the pastor said. "Would you like to go to Viljandi to be with her for a few days? I can manage all right here. You'll be able to visit your parents as well. I'm sure they would be happy to see you and the children."

"Oh Karla, you're an angel. I'll take Tädi with me. I'm sure she would like to see Ema and to visit Jüri's grave."

A few days later, at the end of January 1943, the pastor heard that the news had been confirmed on Finnish radio. Field Marshal Friedrich Paulus had surrendered the entire German Sixth Army, ending the siege of Stalingrad. The tide had turned, as the letter Kingsepp received a day later from an old friend pointed out.

Hjalmar Herne, his classmate and closest friend at Tartu University and now a pastor in Uppsala, wanted to know if Karl and his family would like to move to Sweden. He could arrange for all the necessary papers, he wrote, and there would be a place for Karl as an assistant pastor in a large congregation. Later, he would be sure to have his own church.

His reason for asking, he said, was that it was generally agreed in Sweden that Germany was on the verge of collapsing. America was expected to send troops to Europe any day now, and that would surely spell the doom of Hitler's dream of a thousand-year

Reich. They expected the Soviets to push back the Germans on the Eastern Front and to claim all the German-occupied territories as their own. He didn't think that the Allies would interfere with Russia's push as long as the war was on, and after that it would be too late. He ended his letter with a dire warning:

"Pastors will be targeted again, so it would be best to get out now, while it's possible. If you wait too long, you're likely to end up in the *Gulag.*"

Bless that man, Kingsepp thought. *He's a true friend. But there is no way I can go.*

He was still confident that the Allies would prevent Stalin from re-occupying the Baltic countries. They had done nothing previously to stop Russia' annexation of the Baltic States, so they must be feeling guilty enough to prevent a repeat injustice, he reasoned. It would be premature to leave. He would write back to thank Hjalmar, but decline the offer. When Evely returned from Viljandi a couple of days later, the pastor told her about Hjalmar's kind offer and his decision to turn it down.

Evely couldn't believe her ears, but as usual she tried to temper her words. "Are you sure that was wise, Karla? Everyone I spoke to in Viljandi doubts that the Germans can hold off the Russians and they're already starting to look for escape hatches. Even Hilda. She says if they break through she won't stay here, not without Mark. If they can't have a father, she said, she at least wants her daughters to grow up in a free country. And you know what, Karla? She's right. We also have to consider our children's future. And yours too, of course. You've told me many times that the Reds will be even more bloody-minded if they ever come back. We don't have a future here."

Kingsepp was almost convinced by her words. Had he made a mistake in turning down Hjalmar so quickly? He should have waited to at least talk it over with Evely. Events were picking up speed, faster than he had thought possible. "What does Mati say about how the war is going? He hasn't been sent to the front yet, has he?"

"No, he's still in Tartu, but he told Isa recently that the Reds are almost at the Estonian border and that he expects to be sent to the Narva front any day. He's seen how the Germans operate and he's beginning to regret enlisting. But he admits he probably would have been conscripted anyway. Some of his friends are still hoping to get to Finland. Not much chance of that, though."

"There's a certain irony in that," the pastor said. "I heard that most of our boys who were fighting in Finland are actually trying to get back here to help hold back the Russians."

"Well, that just shows how crazy things are here," Evely said, "and how much we need to leave. Do you think Hjalmar's offer would still be good if you wrote to him again? Now *is* the time to go – before it's too late."

"Let's wait a bit longer, Evely. I can't bear the thought of leaving just yet," her husband said gently. "My mother's here, my brother, your parents and brothers. Everyone we know. Everything we've ever wanted is here."

"But do we want to raise our children under the Reds?" Evely asked. "That's what I can't bear."

Chapter Thirty

The pastor had a second chance to flee the country in the summer of 1944, when Hjalmar, his friend from the university days, again implored him to bring his family to Sweden. This time, Hjalmar sailed to Estonia in a borrowed yacht and appeared without warning on the surprised pastor's doorstep.

"Did you not get my letter?" Hjalmar asked. "I wrote to you and Oskar and Heino, and they got back to me. That's why I came. I just assumed your letter must have been delayed, but I guess you never got mine." The plan, he said, was for him to take the three pastors' families back to Sweden on the small yacht he had borrowed from one of his parishioners. The other pastors were already in Tallinn waiting impatiently for the Kingsepps to join them. They came from parishes much closer to the front and were convinced the Russians could overrun the country in a matter of days. Hjalmar had hurried to Vändra to fetch the Kingsepps so that they could get away quickly.

"I had expected that you would be ready to go when I arrived. But that can't be helped. You'll just have to take what you can because my friend the boat owner is determined to leave today. I think he's already sorry that he agreed to come, because the Russians are flying over the Baltic and shooting at any boats near the coast. He says it's not safe to stay any longer."

Evely looked at Karl imploringly. "This may be our last chance, Karla. We can't afford to miss it."

Karl, however, was strangely reluctant. "I can't," he said. "It's too sudden. I promised everyone I would see the Confirmation class to the end. That's just three more days. We're bound to be safe for at least that long. The Germans and our boys are still holding off the Russians at *Sinimäed*."

"It's not just a question of time, Karl. It's also a matter of means," Hjalmar pointed out. "The Germans are withdrawing and

181

the Russians could easily close the sea lanes by next week. I know how important this Confirmation is to you and your congregation, but is it worth your lives? I'm sure your congregation will understand. You really can't wait any longer, Karl."

Kingsepp didn't seem to be listening as he stared vacantly into space, lost in thought.

"I know what we can do," he suddenly said. "I've got the answer. Evely, you take the children and go with Hjalmar. I'll celebrate Confirmation in three days and then I'll join you in Sweden as soon as I can."

Evely burst into tears. "No, Karl, I won't go without you. Transport is very uncertain; there's a good chance you won't get out if we don't go now. And what would I do there without you? If you won't come with us, then I will also stay. You know what we promised on our wedding day – that we would stay together until death do us part."

Kingsepp was impatient. "Don't be so melodramatic, Evely. Do you think I want to be separated from you? It's only for a few days at most. Then we'll be together again."

Evely started to sob quietly. "No Karla, that's my final answer. I won't go alone."

"I think you're both making a big mistake," Hjalmar said again. "The Reds are going to be here sooner than you think and then they will seal all the ports. This may be your last chance."

"I appreciate all you're doing for us, Hjalmar, but I just can't go now," Kingsepp said. "Don't worry. I expect to see you in a week or so to thank you again for all your help."

Hjalmar smiled wanly. "If that's what you want, then so be it. I really do hope, for all your sakes, that you are right. I have to go now; the others are waiting. God save you, my friend."

Evely was angry after Hjalmar left. "What's this sudden importance of Confirmation Day? When the Russians were here, you couldn't even hold a Confirmation class, and everybody survived. No one's going to criticize you for leaving now. You know very well that they'd all do the same if they were in your shoes. And you don't have to visit your mother. She's already told you she doesn't expect to see you again. I love my parents, too, but I'm ready to leave without saying goodbye, if necessary. They'll understand that it's for the good of the children. Besides, it doesn't have to be forever. Who knows what's going to happen? After the war is over, we may be back here more quickly than you think."

She kept looking at him with armor-piercing eyes, trying to win him over by sheer will power. "Please, Karla, for all our sakes ... please run after him and tell him you've reconsidered. Please, for the children's sake."

Kingsepp had never seen his wife so distraught. It hurt him to see her like that and for a moment he considered doing as she wished. But something he couldn't explain held him back.

Two months ago, the pastor had had an extraordinary dream, more vivid than any he could remember since he had been a boy. It was as if he were watching a movie. A horseman, mounted on a pure white charger, was riding pell-mell into battle, waving a mighty broadsword. As the horseman galloped closer to the hillock where a crowd of young men were milling about in confusion, the pastor could see that the rider looked like Lembit. But this was not the proud strong warrior depicted by the statue in Suure-Jaani so admired by Estonian patriots; this Lembit was hollow-cheeked, wraith-like, with bloody wounds all over his upper body. The pastor, who suddenly found himself standing in front of the crowd of young men, was sure that he was about to be run down, but at the last minute Lembit pulled up and without a word handed his blood-stained sword to the pastor. Kingsepp, who didn't want to take it, felt himself gripping it before he could resist. As he looked down at his hands ruefully, he saw that what he was clasping was not the sword, but a cross. When he looked up again, no one was there. He was alone in the parish church, waiting for his people.

Since then the dream had recurred several times, usually a night or two before he met with his Confirmation class. He had never believed in dreams or omens but somehow couldn't resist the emotional pull of this dream. Was his subconscious mind telling him something – that it was his duty to prepare his congregation for the impending takeover by the Reds? He couldn't help but be reminded of *Quo Vadis?* the novel he had read as a boy, which had had a huge impact on his decision to become a pastor. Like St. Peter in that book, was he being prodded to rethink his priorities and commitments? He didn't quite know what to make of it, but he knew he would feel foolish telling anyone that he was staying because of a dream. Better to remain quiet and follow his heart.

"I just can't, Evely," he finally managed to say. "Believe me, I wouldn't do anything that would put you or the children in danger. But I have to stay; this is something I just know I have to do – for my congregation, and for my own sake. I know that God will see us through this safely. I feel that I have His word on it."

They looked at each other for a long time, not speaking. Finally, in even tones, Evely said, "So tell me, Karla, what's your plan? God helps those who help themselves, you always say. So tell me exactly, how are we going to help ourselves now?"

"I don't know yet, but I have faith. God will show us a way."

Evely looked at him with sad eyes. Without saying another word, she turned and left the room.

Chapter Thirty-One

Confirmation Day, or *Leeripäev*, was usually a festive time, a celebration of a rite of passage that helped knit together families and the community in the common values that would sustain the parish for years to come.

It was, of course, primarily a religious celebration, the reception into the congregation of freshly-minted Christians, who had followed a comprehensive twelve-week course of instruction in the beliefs and procedures of the Lutheran church. The pastor provided the young *leerilapsed* with an overview of the Old Testament and guided them through a reading of the New Testament accounts of Christ's life and teachings. They learned by heart their confession of faith, the congregation's responses during the liturgy, the Ten Commandments, the Lord's Prayer and several hymns meant to bolster their faith should they ever have to confront a dark night of the soul.

But it was simultaneously a secular celebration of the renewal of the community, the coming of age of a new generation to carry on the values and traditions of their forefathers and mothers. What the congregation saw entering the church on Confirmation Sunday were several dozen nervous-looking boys and girls of sixteen and seventeen, decked out in store-bought suits or long white dresses lovingly sewn for them by their mothers and grandmothers. Pinned to their chests were the corsages and boutonnieres of red or pink carnations, specially cultivated for the occasion by members of the congregation. Leaving the church, they were no longer children, but young men and women, ready to take their place as fully-fledged members of the congregation. No longer nervous or hesitant, they walked out confidently and proudly, secure in the knowledge that they were now adults in the eyes of their parents and their community.

In reality, not much would change for most of them. The majority had already been working long, hard days alongside their parents on the family farm, and would continue to do so. Fewer than half would finish secondary school, and from that group only a privileged few would get a post-secondary education. A small number of them, mostly younger sons, might take up an apprenticeship in some trade or find work in a nearby town. A few of the girls would get married within two or three years to older men, who had already taken over their family farms; others would wait for their loved one to inherit farms or would move to an urban center to find jobs in factories or as a domestics. Some had no prospects at all. But none of that mattered for the time being; this day was meant to be celebrated by all.

This year, however, there was a different, edgier feel to the day – an undercurrent of fear of what the future might bring. For the second time in four years, Russian forces were closing in, and everyone was all too aware that some of the fresh, young faces in the church that day would find an early grave while fighting to defend their country.

Regardless of their concerns about the future, they were determined to make the most of what might turn out to be the last *Leeripäev* in Vändra. They would do their best to have a joyful celebration – like it had always been. It would be a time for the stops to be pulled out and for people to enjoy themselves to the full – before the deluge.

Most families, with the encouragement of the pastor, had sent all their children who were within two or three years of the customary age to the Confirmation class. It was the largest class the pastor had ever taught, 72 young adults ranging in age from 14 to 20. The pastor had committed himself to completing an expanded course of instruction and had worked diligently over the past twelve weeks to ensure that they would remember their Christian heritage, no matter what the future brought. And he had been determined to be there to bless them, even if it meant risking his chance to get away before the Russians made their final push. The church had to be renewed, he told himself. He had this final duty to fulfill.

186

For the first time in two years, the pastor had instructed the elderly sexton to ring the church bells as loudly and for as long as he felt able. "This may be the last time for a long while that this will be possible," the pastor told Arno Salu that morning. "Let's make it a memorable day." "I will be glad to do it for the *leerilapsed*," Arno said with tears in his eyes, "and also for my poor son Randar, who always loved ringing the bells before he went astray."

As he stood before the congregation that morning, the pastor was smiling broadly. What a heartwarming sight, he thought: All those tall, handsome boys, standing stiffly in their adult clothes, with their hair slicked back, from time to time glancing up from their shoes to look around them with shy grins; and the bright-eyed girls, who had cast off their pinafores for long white dresses, looking mature beyond their years, their hair no longer loose or in braids, but upswept or in ladylike curls, some even showing discreet traces of makeup. Soon they would be standing before the altar of God and in front of their community to recite in unison the creed that for the rest of their lives was meant to be their guiding star.

After professing their faith, the Confirmation class was ready to receive the sacrament of Holy Communion for the first time. As the pastor blessed and distributed the bread and the wine, he felt an intense joy, as though the Holy Spirit had descended upon them all. As he passed among the youths kneeling at the altar railing, he looked deeply into their eyes and saw only hope and joy. No harm would befall them. Everything would turn out all right.

> "May the Lord bless you and keep you;
> May His face shine upon you
> and be gracious unto you;
> May He lift up His countenance upon you
> and give you peace."

As he made the sign of the cross to complete his blessing the pastor felt happy – as happy as he had ever been, he thought. Evely, sitting in her front row pew, still smarting from what she considered to be her husband's irresponsibility, was struck by the beatific look on his face. This is why he stayed, she thought. He mightn't have communicated it to her very well, but obviously he had felt that staying behind to carry out this final pastoral duty was a necessary act of redemption ... for him ... and for the whole community.

She felt happy for him, and thought she could almost forgive him for not leaving when they had had the opportunity. But then the image of her children flashed into her mind.

As the organist started the recessional, she looked around at the hubbub surrounding her. Parents and relatives were rushing towards the *leerilapsed* with bouquets of flowers, shouting out their congratulations. She was in no mood to mingle with the celebrants, Evely decided, as she slipped out quietly to make her way home. The First Act of the day's drama had come to an end.

Act Two required a change of scenery. Relatives and friends, several of whom had had to wait outside the overflowing church, escorted the youths with their armloads of flowers to family gatherings at their individual homes. There, the traditional presents of a locket or a pocket watch would be given, and proud parents would serve the best dinner they could afford. Weeks of work would have gone into the preparation of traditional foods -- *rosolje, skumbria, sült, hapukapsad, seenesoust, kringel* – which would accompany roasted meat and potato dishes. Homemade beer, vodka, tea and cranberry juice would be refreshments.

Act Three would begin some hours later, when groups of youths would reconvene at previously designated houses, to carry on the festivities with dancing and singing well into the early hours. That part, the pastor thought ruefully, sometimes got out of hand, often because adults, who should know better, even some of the parents, would press drinks on the newly-confirmed youngsters. "You're adults now," they'd say. "You can have a drink," and they'd hand the youth a glass with a hearty *"Prosit."* But he wasn't about to criticize anyone, the pastor thought. Who knows what tomorrow would bring? Let them enjoy themselves while they could.

At some homes, however, there would be no celebrations. The thoughts of families like the Maasiks and the Jürissons would instead turn to some lonely outpost in the *Gulag* or to a heaped mound of earth in some shell-pocked battlefield. Vändra had lost nearly 300 of its men and women in the past four years, and it was the homes of their grieving families that the pastor particularly wanted to visit. It would have been impossible to visit them all on Confirmation Day, so he had spent the last week making pastoral visits to most of those homes, leaving only a few of the most recently bereaved families to be called on that day. He was tired from the long service in the morning and didn't look forward to the bone-jarring rides to the far-flung homes, but he was determined to offer consolation and say prayers where he believed they would be most needed.

Toivo Maasik, the student who had written an essay critical of the Soviet regime, should have been among the leerilapsed, but instead was languishing in a Siberian work camp. His mother had not attended the ceremony in church. "I know I should have gone there to pray for him, but I couldn't face seeing all his friends there and Toivo somewhere off in Siberia or worse," she told the pastor. "All I could manage to do was to sit in my bedroom with the curtains closed and cry. I must have frightened Veljo because he just sat in the corner of the room and cried all day, too. He never mentions his brother's name, but he keeps asking all the time about his daddy. I don't know what to tell him. Ever since the Germans conscripted my Taavi and sent him to the front, I've had no news from him. They say there were really heavy casualties at Velikiye Luki. If he's... Oh Pastor, what am I going to do?"

The pastor's heart went out to the distraught woman whose husband and oldest son had both been taken from her. He was about to say a prayer, but he noticed young Veljo staring hungrily at the larder. "Have you had anything to eat yet today?" he asked Mrs. Maasik, who shook her head listlessly. "Will I make you some tea and a sandwich? That's all I know how to make," he added apologetically.

Getting no response, he started rifling through the larder for the wherewithal for fixing a sandwich. Twenty minutes later, he gently took Mrs. Maasik by the elbow and steered her to the kitchen table where three steaming mugs of tea and a plate of sliced pork sandwichs were waiting. Six-year-old Veljo needed no urging but dug in right away. The pastor, who had planned to say grace, just smiled and offered him another sandwich. There would be time enough for a prayer after they had eaten. By the time the pastor left, both Veljo and his mother were feeling better. The pastor's sandwichs had removed some of the bleakness from their lives and Mrs. Maasik was consoled by the pastor's prayers for her missing loved ones. "I don't know what God's will is for them, but now I feel that He's at least looking after them," she told him, as he was leaving.

He had finished making his rounds, but there was one more home he had to visit, that of Peeter Kallas, the chairman of the church council, whose 14-year-old daughter Aimi had been the youngest member of the Confirmation class. Peeter had gone to Tallinn a few days ago, hinting that he might have some good news to share when he got back. He, too, had missed the boat, so to speak, and was looking for other avenues by which to leave Estonia before the Russians arrived. If anyone could find such a way, the pastor was convinced, it would be Peeter.

Chapter Thirty-Two

The Kallas family lived a few kilometers outside the village, in a large company house close to the linen factory which Peeter managed. Despite the grandeur of the house and grounds, Peeter was a serious, cerebral man who chose to live simply and quietly. He was punctilious in his attention to his business during the day, but in the evenings, after dinner, he liked nothing better than to make himself comfortable in an armchair in his study and dip into one of the works of philosophy, theology, history or biography that he had accumulated over the years. He had few other indulgences, but they were always of the highest quality, like the Arabian coffee he imported himself. Lunch at his house would have been a treat, but the pastor had declined the invitation in order to be with the bereaved families. His plan, he said, was to make Peeter's house his last stop, which would enable them to have a longer conversation.

When he arrived at the Kallas's house, Peeter, who was expecting the pastor, met him at the door. "Thank you for coming, Pastor. I know how much this day means to you and how busy you've been. I think I can speak for the entire parish and certainly for the church council when I say that this was a day that will be remembered for a very long time."

As Peeter spoke, he noticed the pastor's eyes misting over and quickly moved on to say that there was a pot of coffee being kept warm in the kitchen for him. "I know how much you love a good cup, so let me get it and then we can have the chat I promised you." When he came back with two steaming china cups and two slices of *kringel*, he suggested they sit outside in a quiet nook of the garden. "I was actually hoping to talk to you this morning, but you were too busy. So let me tell you now that I've come across some potentially good news." The pastor's ears perked up. There was only one kind of good news for most people these days.

"As you know, the reason I was away was to arrange passage for my family to go to Sweden this week, but that didn't work out. Like you, I had left it too late. Getting a ship out of Tallinn is impossible now. Everyone expects that the Russians will occupy the city in another day or two. The captain of the ship I was hoping to go on had already left. He was afraid of being torpedoed by the Russians, I was told. I can't really blame him. You've heard, of course, what happened to the *Moero*? Imagine, they actually sank a hospital ship. More than 600 people drowned! Nevertheless, I had hoped that someone, somewhere was still preparing to go, so I spent several days looking around for other ships, but I had no luck."

Peeter took a sip of his coffee. "But I didn't put all my eggs in one basket. I had another reason to go to Tallinn. A week ago, Toivo, our company mechanic, told me that he had looked more carefully at an old, broken-down three-wheeled pickup truck that had been rusting away in a shed for years. Toivo thought he might be able to get it running if we could somehow find some tires and a few parts for the engine. That's the other reason why I went to Tallinn, and took Toivo with me. I have an old school friend who teaches in the technical school there and I thought that between them, he and Toivo might be able to figure out some way to get the truck going."

Peeter paused for another sip. "It was a long shot, so I didn't want to mention it to anyone, not even to my family. But given the circumstances, I didn't want to leave any stone unturned. Well, it turned out that Viktor, my friend, was a hoarder and had several kinds of old tires and all sorts of mechanical bits lying around in their machine shop. Anyway, to make a long story short, while I was out looking for a ship, the two of them were able to cannibalize and retool the bits we needed, so that we should have all the missing parts. The tires were the trickiest part. There were only two that fit the truck, but Toivo was able to find another rim for the front axle so that it would take a slightly smaller motorcycle tire. The tires are all quite bald, but he figured they should be good for one last trip, if we don't hit a sharp rock or anything like that.

"We managed to bring all the stuff back with us, and Toivo is now working like a demon to put it all together. If everything works as planned, we'll be ready to leave tomorrow or the next day. It's cutting things fine, but if we can get to Saaremaa, I heard there is a German ship still there, probably the last one, that's evacuating their officers and administrators. There should be room for us, if only we can get there in time. Right now, I can't promise that – as you know, the port is more than 200 kilometers from here and the roads may be blocked in places – but are you willing to give it a try?"

"Of course!" the flabbergasted pastor replied. He had been on the brink of resigning himself to living under Soviet occupation again or, God forbid, in the woods if it came to that. So even the slim chance that was being offered sounded like music to his ears. "That's incredible news, Peeter. Thanks be to God, and thanks to you, too, of course. I was starting to fear that I had made a very bad choice in not leaving with my friend Hjalmar. Not so much for my sake, but for the children and Evely. But I can see now that I should not have doubted that God would see us through to safety."

"Amen to that," Peeter said.

After Peeter had finished filling in the details, the pastor rose to go. "Thank you once again, Peeter. Thanks for everything. I better go now and tell Evely. I'm afraid she hasn't been happy with me these days. We'll also have a lot to do if we're leaving tomorrow or the next day."

On the way home, he kept thinking how happy Evely would be to hear this news. She hadn't been very communicative the past week and had avoided him for most of that time, saying she needed to look after the children. They hadn't had a real talk since he had turned down Hjalmar's last offer of help. Today, he had hoped she would accompany him to some of the celebrations after the Confirmation service, but she had rushed back to the manse before he had even had time to change out of his cassock.

When Karl arrived back at the manse, Evely was feeding the baby while simultaneously trying to stop the toddlers from quarrelling over a toy. "Can you take care of Jaak and Annely?" she asked rather testily. "Tädi's lying down with a headache and I can't manage all three of them.

"What are you so happy about anyway?" she asked, after noticing the huge smile on her husband's face as he lifted up and hugged his children. "One would think you've found a way out of here. But we're stuck, and we'll just have to make the best of it."

"But that's just it! We might have a way out after all. If Peeter Kallas can get his truck working by tomorrow, we can still catch a ship."

The excitement in his voice finally reached through to Evely. "Are you serious, Karla? What truck are you talking about? Mr. Kallas really has a truck?"

"Well, yes... I mean maybe. It's an old wreck, but his mechanic Toivo thinks he can get it running by tomorrow or the next day. Once it's going, we have to leave right away."

Evely suddenly came alive, throwing dozens of questions at her husband without waiting for his answers. "Hold on," he said. "If you give me a chance, I'll tell you everything I know. First of all, it's a very old and a very small three-wheeled truck. Toivo will be the driver, but he is single, and there are only three in Peeter's family, so there will be space for all of us if we hold the children on our laps. There won't be room for anything more than one or two small cases under the seats or on the roof of the cab, so we can't take much. Peeter says we won't need to pay for the passage if they let us on, but we might need to bribe people to get that far. No one wants German or Russian money, he says, so we have to take whatever else we have that's valuable."

"I'd go with just the clothes on our backs, if that's what it takes to get away from here," Evely said, scurrying off to get her rather empty-looking jewelery box. "I don't know how far these things will get us," she said, "but I'll bring them all. The only thing I want to keep is my wedding band."

"There won't be much room for anything else once we pack the children's things and a change of clothes for us," she added, "and we'll need some food and water, I guess. But I'd like to bring a few family photographs. They won't take up any space." They spent the evening anxiously waiting for word from Peeter Kallas, and packing and repacking their small cases to see what else they might squeeze in. Neither of them slept much.

The next morning, while still waiting to hear about the truck, they spent tearful hours saying goodbye to friends and neighbors, who started dropping by as soon as word of their possible departure got out. "What a stroke of luck to find that old truck," Mr. Männik said. "If anyone deserves that, it's surely you."

The pastor had hurriedly convened a meeting to say goodbye to the members of the church council and to discuss arrangements they might make in his absence. Several retired pastors and theology professors, he told them, were already planning to cover for the younger pastors who had left. One of them would be available once a month to conduct a church service and perform funerals, for as long as the churches remained open. After leading them in a brief prayer for the survival of the church, the pastor thanked them all for making his years in Vändra so memorable. He had managed to keep his composure, but his voice broke when he came to Mr. Männik who, he said, was the real heart and soul of the parish and deserved not only his thanks, but the thanks of the entire congregation for his many years of exceptional service. As the pastor prepared to leave the church, the councillors lined up to shake his hand. It was a shame that it had had to come to this, they said, but they agreed that, after the way he had been targeted by the Reds, he had no choice but to go. All of them said they would pray for him and his family.

"I don't know why, but I have a feeling in my bones that you'll be back before you know it," Mr. Männik told him as the two men walked back to the manse. "At least I hope so, because you're the best pastor we've ever had, at least in my lifetime. And don't worry about anything; I'll keep everything shipshape while you're away."

Back at the rectory, Kingsepp found a tearful Hilda Soosaar, who had come in on her day off to say goodbye. "I'm going to miss you, Pastor. God bless you and yours." Even stolid old Jukku's eyes were moist as he haltingly promised to look after the church farm "just the way the pastor wanted me to do it."

Overcome with emotion, the pastor excused himself to go to his office, where for a long time he sat mournfully behind his desk before picking up his pen to write to his mother and brother, his uncle and all the friends he would not be able to see before departing. The letters were hard to write. *I feel like a convict writing my last words on the eve before my execution,* he thought. *All I can say is that I love them and am sustained by the hope that we'll meet again one way or another.* "God bless us all," he wrote in signing off.

Evely, meanwhile, had also been busy writing letters to her parents and brothers, promising to stay in touch wherever they ended up. Tädi, with whom Evely had developed as strong a bond as with her own parents, meanwhile paced the floor anxiously, waiting for the children to wake from their naps. "Poor little chicks," she lamented. "I wonder where they'll find a bed the next few days."

"You really must come with us, Tädi," Evely said for the umpteenth time. "You'll be on your own if you stay, and the children will be devastated without you. There has to be room for you in the truck."

"No, Karl said there isn't any room; besides I want to stay here, so I can be buried beside Jüri," Tädi answered, less than convincingly. As Tädi busied herself tending to the children, who had just woken up in cranky moods, Evely could see that she was already feeling lost. "They really love you Tädi, especially the baby. I think you should get a bag ready, and we'll squeeze you in, even if we have to leave something behind. Please?"

Time passed very slowly for them. By mid-afternoon, there had been no word from Peeter and they were beginning to hear the sound of artillery firing from the direction of Tallinn. "That's the Russians advancing," Jukku said. He and many others had remained in front of the manse waiting to say a final goodbye. "You'll have to make a run for it, even if you leave now," he said.

The ever-helpful Mr. Männik, who had gone off a while ago, returned now to give them an update on the state of the roads. The retreating Germans had blown up several bridges to delay the Russian advance, he said, including one that they needed to cross to get to the Baltic coast. "There is another possibility," Mr. Männik said. "You'll have to go several kilometers out of your way, but there's an uncharted ford that some of the local farmers use. It's hard to find if you don't know about it but you shouldn't have any trouble with this," he said pointing out the route on a small map he had brought. "There's about 30 centimeters of water there, but the flat stones underneath will provide a good footing."

Just when everyone was starting to think that it was all for nothing, the three-wheeler arrived with a clatter, belching black smoke. The downturned faces brightened up and there was a

196

collective sigh of relief and even some cheering. On board were Toivo and the three members of the Kallas family. The pastor, who had been prevailed upon by Evely, rushed over to the truck and spoke quietly to Peeter Kallas, who nodded.

"Come on, Tädi," the pastor shouted. "We can't afford to waste any time. Here, I'll help you up." Tears streaming down her cheeks, Tädi squeezed in between Evely and Mrs. Kallas, who was sitting beside her daughter Aimi. It was a tight fit in the back, but with the three older women each holding a child, they managed it. The pastor and Peeter squeezed into the cab beside Toivo.

Even the pastor seemed to be struck speechless as the truck rattled off; like the others, he wiped away his tears and tried to smile as he waved to well-wishers who had stayed to say goodbye. As they clattered through the village, dozens more people came out on their doorsteps to wave and shout "Head reisu" and "Jumal kaasa." "We'll miss you, Pastor. Come back as soon as you can," several of them shouted, causing more tears to well up in his eyes. Dozens of youngsters ran alongside the truck, shouting goodbyes until they reached the edge of the village, where they continued to wave until the truck disappeared around a bend.

Only a few kilometers down the road the truck shuddered and came to a sudden stop. "Don't worry," Toivo said, "at least not yet. I anticipated that some adjustments would be necessary along the way." After a bit of fiddling around under the hood, he managed to restart the engine. "It may do this from time to time," he said, "but I can deal with it."

About two kilometers from the ford, they unexpectedly ran into a small column of Russian soldiers marching towards them, with whom they would have to share the road for almost three hundred meters. "Let me do the talking," Peeter told the pastor. "I think I can speak enough Russian to convince them we're on their side." Luckily, their route to the ford had temporarily caused them to drive away from the coast and back towards central Estonia, so the soldiers didn't seem too interested in them. "They probably think we are going to Tallinn to welcome the Red Army," the pastor whispered to Peeter.

They had nearly passed the column, when a soldier near the rear started to amuse his companions by making lewd comments about Aimi, the Kallas's pretty teenage daughter sitting in the open back of the truck. Maybe she would like to join him for a picnic, he suggested. It might have ended badly but for Evely, who had gone to primary school in Russia when her father had worked for the Tsarist railroad. In a loud, angry voice, she started scolding the soldier for his rude comments about "my daughter," causing an officer to approach and apologize for the soldier's misbehavior. He'd had too much to drink, the officer said, and wished them a safe journey.

"It's a good thing we met them where we did and not while we're heading towards the coast. If they had thought we were fleeing and wanted to search us, we would have been finished," Peeter told the pastor after they had crossed the ford. "I think we owe it all to your wife. The way she berated that soldier stopped him in his tracks, and her Russian is so good they may even have thought we were Russians."

They didn't meet up with any more patrols on the way to the coast and were making good time when they had two mechanical breakdowns in quick succession, followed by a blowout in one of the tires. Despite the anxiety this occasioned, Toivo, who had strapped a tube-patching kit and an air pump onto the hood, was able to cope with them all. Luckily, too, the ferry to Saaremaa was still operating when they reached the coast, and they were able to cross fairly quickly.

On the island, however, with another 75 kilometers to travel to the port near Kuressaare, they suddenly ran out of gas. The men hurriedly fanned out to comb the small town near the ferry harbor for gasoline. Toivo came back to say that he had found German soldiers guarding a fuel depot, but they were reluctant to sell him any gasoline.

Peeter said he had an idea. He climbed up to the roof of the cab where his suitcases were tied down and after a few minutes came down carrying a small package. "Come with me," he told Toivo and the pastor. At the depot, Peeter explained to the soldiers that he was helping a highly-respected Lutheran pastor to flee from the communists who wanted to arrest him and his family. He then introduced Kingsepp, who spoke briefly but movingly in German about his hope that they would help his family escape from their common enemy, the Red Army. Peeter then unwrapped his package, revealing two bottles of high quality vodka, which he said he wanted the soldiers to have as a token of appreciation for their help.

The soldiers looked at each other. One of them shrugged and reached for the bottles. The other one went behind the linked wire fence and came back with a 10-liter jerry can. *"Dankeschõõn,"* they all said to the soldiers before hurrying off. "Works every time," Peeter told the others as soon as they were out of earshot.

When they reached the harbor at Roomassaare, three or four kilometers outside Kuressaare, they were greatly relieved to see a large troop carrier anchored offshore. As they got closer they noticed that the ship looked deserted and that there was none of the activity on the pier that indicated a ship was about to embark.Toivo pulled up beside what used to be the harbormaster's building and got out to look for someone to tell him what was going on. When he came back, he looked a little perplexed.

"The good news is that there is room for everyone who is here now. But the ship was hit yesterday afternoon by an incendiary bomb from a Russian plane. The fire is out now, but some repairs are necesary and there are some toxic gases they have to ventilate, but they expect to get going tomorrow night. Meanwhile they're not allowing anyone on board. There are no facilities here, so most people have gone back to Kuressaare where they can sleep on the floor in some of the schools. They told me we should go back there also. Anyway, they're going to need every available vehicle to bring everyone back tomorrow, so I've been conscripted for that."

When the ship left the following evening, September 30, 1944, it was carrying nearly 2,000 evacuees. After shuttling back and forth all day between Kuressaare and Roomassaare, Toivo just made it on board by the skin of his teeth. He had had a flat tire just after starting on his last run back with only two passengers, both young men who had gallantly insisted that women and children should go first. The three had abandoned the truck and started running when they heard the ship's all-clear whistle.

"It was God's hand that saved us," Toivo told the pastor later. Just when they thought all was lost, one of the young men found a rack of abandoned bicycles. Pedalling recklessly through the deserted streets, they got to the pier just as a man and a woman in a small boat started rowing frantically to the ship. After jamming on the brakes at the edge of the pier, Toivo and his two companions made flying leaps into the water while shouting at the rowers to stop. Luckily they did, and sailors on the ship, who had heard their shouts, threw down a rope ladder so they could all clamber aboard.

It was dusk by the time the ship pulled away from the harbor. All the Estonians who could find a spot crowded onto the deck to watch the shore recede from view. Everyone, the pastor saw, kept their eyes fixed for as long as possible on the homeland they might never see again. With tears streaming down his face, the pastor quietly started singing the Estonian Anthem, which was immediately picked up by Evely and several people standing nearby. Soon they were all singing with hushed, sometimes faltering voices. Tears were streaming down every face as they sang the third verse of the Estonian National Anthem:

> *"Su üle Jumal valvaku, Mu kallis isamaa;*
> *Ta olgu sinu kaitseja, Ja võtku rohkest õnnista*
> *Mis iial ette võtad sa, Mu kallis isamaa."*

> "May God watch over you, My dear fatherland;
> May He protect you, And bless you
> in all that you undertake, My dear fatherland."

The End

Glossary of some Estonian words and phrases used in this book

Ema	Mother
Gümnaasium	Secondary school
Hapukapsad	Sauerkraut
Head reisu	(Have a) good trip
Härra	Mister or Sir
Hiis	A sacred oak grove for Taara ceremonies
Isa	Father
Jumal kaasa	God be with you
Jõgi	River
Kalevipoeg	Estonian epic national poem
Kaitseliit	Home Guard militia
Karjapoisid	Pre-teen herd-boys
Kringel	Sweet, breadlike cake, in the shape of a pretzel
Kurat	Literally "devil" – an all-purpose swear word; "Kuradi" is the adjective
Laulupidu	Choral song festival
Leerilapsed	Children who are being Confirmed
Leeripäev	Confirmation Day
Metsa Talu	Forest Farm
Metsavennad	Brothers of the forest (partisan guerrillas)
Mõis	Manor house or country estate of the Baltic German gentry; "Mõisad" is the plural
Oktooberfest	Oktoberfest
Rosolje	Beet and potato salad
Rukki leib	Rye bread
Sinimäed	"Blue Mountains" – a series of hills west of Narva where Estonian soldiers and remnants of the German army held back the advancing Soviet Red Army, allowing time for many Estonian civilians to escape
Saun	Estonian for the Finnish "sauna"

Sea praad	Pork roast
Seenesoust	Mushroom sauce
Skumbria	Smoked mackerel, from the Polish tradition
Soome Poiss	"Finnish Boy" - an Estonian volunteer soldier who fought with the Finns in the Winter War against the Russians in 1939-40, "Soome Poisid" in the plural
Sült	Jellied veal with horseraddish sauce
Taara usk	A druid-like form of panhtheism that was the ancient Estonians' folk religion
Tädi	Aunt
Tere	Hello
Tere, Pastori Härra	Hello, Pastor Sir